Tunnel Through Time

by LESTER DEL REY

Illustrated by HAL FRENCK

SCHOLASTIC BOOK SERVICES
NEW YORK · TORONTO · LONDON · AUCKLAND · SYDNEY

Another book by Lester del Rey
available from Scholastic Book Services
The Runaway Robot

Copyright © 1966 by Lester del Rey. This edition is published by Scholastic
Book Services, a division of Scholastic Magazines, Inc., by arrangement with
The Westminster Press.

17 16 15 14 13 12 11 10 9 8   6 7 8 9/7 01/8

Printed in the U.S.A.

Contents

Of Time and Dinosaurs

I KNEW THERE WAS SOMETHING in the wind from the way
they were talking there after dinner — Dad and Doctor
Tom. I sensed it from knowing Dad — he's been my father
for more than seventeen years — I'll be eighteen in three
months. And then as I came into the room, Doctor Tom
said, "If it's money, I can help. I have an unused appropriation I could swing — Oh, hello, Bob."

He meant me. I'm Bob Miller. "Anything I shouldn't
hear?" I asked.

"Not at all," Dad said. "We were talking about dinosaurs."

"And this unused appropriation: is Doc Tom going to
use it to buy one?"

"Not exactly," Dad said. "We were debating the reasons for their extinction."

I'd been helping Grace, our housekeeper, carry the dishes into the kitchen, so I hadn't been in on the first part of it. But I had a hunch it hadn't been all dinosaurs. I know Dad, and there was something more than casualness in his attitude.

I was pretty proud of him, but he's a guy who is very easy to be proud of. He's a physicist, and he was heading up a team at Benson University on time research. The team was under a grant from the Hellman Foundation, and it was a real top-secret operation.

Actually it wasn't Dad's theory, but he was figured as the best man in the country to work on it. It had to do with the notion that time and gravity are somehow mixed up together, and Russia was known to be doing intensive work on the gravity riddle.

If Russia came up with a means of negating gravity and eliminating boosters on its space stuff, we would be the last team in the second division, and that had the big boys worried.

Of course there were other teams working on the same problem, and Dad wasn't bound to hold to that line. He could go anywhere that his nose led him inside the broad boundaries of time itself.

And I had a hunch he'd gone someplace.

"I always thought the dinos faded out because mammals came along and ate their eggs," I said.

"Fried or scrambled?" Doc Tom asked innocently.

"Soft-boiled," I told him.

Dad didn't react to the so-called jokes. He had that

look he always wore when he was thinking about one thing and talking about another. "The mammals were around a million years before the dinosaurs began diminishing," he said. But I knew dinos weren't even in his mind. I called him on it, which I was always privileged to do. We had a pretty good relationship, Dad and I.

"But what do the bronts and the dinos have to do with time?" I asked.

Dad peered intently at nothing — another of his predictable traits. When he spoke, he was talking more to himself than to us.

"Did it ever occur to you," he said, "that whatever happens, happens all the time?"

"I don't get it," I said, being honest if nothing else.

"It's a little difficult to explain, Bob, but think of it this way. We look through a telescope and see the explosion of a star."

"That I can understand."

"All right, but for all we know that star could really have exploded a billion years ago."

"Uh-huh. And we're just getting the news because we're so far away."

"Doesn't that suggest an absolute integration of time and distance?"

"Sure but —"

"What I mean is this: Suppose you get down on the floor right now and start doing push-ups. You'd be doing them here at this exact moment. But inject distance and the speed of light. Then go out in space a million light-years and give someone a telescope strong enough to see you and you'd still be doing your push-ups."

"But I'd be pretty tired by then," I grinned.

"This theoretically demonstrable gambit could be carried on into infinity," my father continued. "Therefore, you would go on doing push-ups into eternity."

"Unless," Doc Tom cut in, "we live in a closed system and not in infinity, as some new discoveries indicate."

He was referring to the exciting new "blue galaxy" discoveries that were changing a lot of basic thinking here and there around the scientific world.

"Rather deep thinking for a paleontologist," I kidded. Which was what Doctor Tom was — and also a very good friend.

Doc Tom was forty, but his grin always made him look years younger, and tended to cloud the fact that he was one of the top brains in his field. Not as *top* as Dad, but he came close.

"Deep, maybe," he said, "but also very disturbing. It means that the dinosaurs are still lumbering over the earth. I'd like very much to see one, but to do it I'd have to find a good telescope and plod a few million light-years out into space."

"Perhaps not," Dad said.

His two quiet words were like little bolts of electricity crackling through the room. Neither Doc Tom nor I said anything. We waited.

Dad was silent also, and while I sat there I had a little time to think about things I should have thought about oftener: how lucky I was to have him; how much he'd given me; how he'd been both a father and a mother since I was three years old, when we'd lost Mom. Of course it hadn't been until years later that I realized how hard her death had hit him. But I think he knew that I did understand.

"It's almost impossible to outline even the concept," he growled. "Semantics are mankind's prison. We suffer from lack of tools with which to communicate."

"I'd say the theory negates itself," Doc Tom observed. "It extends an impossibility: that a man could observe the workings of a scene before his own birth. That he could function before his own existence."

"The theory is not new," Dad said, "and that point has always been the great barrier blocking practical application."

We had nothing to say, and after a few moments Dad made a decision. He slapped the arm of his chair with an open palm and got to his feet. "A picture is worth a thousand words," he said. "And I can show you more than a picture. Come with me."

We lived on Faculty Row at the university, and Dad's laboratory was in the Science Building, a short five-minute walk away. But the five minutes seemed like an hour to me as we hurried along.

The laboratory, where Dad and his three assistants worked, was a clean, shining place. I always thought it looked like the kitchen of a modern hotel dining room, although I'd never seen one. But the point was Dad was a stickler for neatness and order. He always said that a sloppy shop indicated a sloppy mind, but I never met enough inventors and research people to know whether he was right or not.

He led us through to what was the back room of the laboratory, a bare place about thirty feet square. There was nothing in it but a square ten-foot platform in the middle — about a foot off the floor — and a panel of controls near the entrance.

There was a metal ring about seven feet in diameter mounted in the center of the raised platform. It looked like the kind that is set fire to and has tigers jumping through it at a circus.

Dad stood by the panel and looked at the platform. "There it is," he said.

Doc Tom eyed the metal ring dubiously. "Uh-huh. It's great. But what is it?"

"What we were talking about."

Doc Tom shrugged. "O.K., but it doesn't look like a dinosaur to me. A dinosaur is —"

"It's a machine," Dad said, "that will allow you to look at your prehistoric beasties firsthand — " Dad's eyes twinkled here — "I hope."

Doc Tom blinked. "You *hope*. Well, that sounds encouraging."

"A time machine," Dad said, "although it isn't a machine at all. Not in the sense that it's a vehicle to carry a time traveler. About the best I can give you by way of explaining it is that is condenses time — tunnels through it, so to speak. That is, I hope it does."

Doc Tom was walking around the platform, peering at the big hoop. His expression was pensive. "We seem to have all the hope we need," he muttered. "How about the faith and charity?"

Dad smiled. "You will provide the faith if all goes well. And the charity? We discussed that earlier. You said you had some unallocated funds."

"Then it's not finished?"

"Not quite. As yet, there are certain bugs."

"Such as?"

"I'm sure it will function — that is, it will deliver a man back into time. But exactly where he will land is another matter."

"You mean he could arrive in yesterday or in a time span where nothing in the way of a world existed?"

"Not quite that. The machine is calibrated and responded to all tests. You might think of it as functioning in hops — long steps back into time. Each hop will double the length of the previous one as momentum is gained. The first one estimates at approximately 10,000 years. If the device continues to function properly, the succeeding ones should be 20,000, then 40,000 and 80,000."

I stood there taking it all in, saying nothing. Doc Tom was circling the platform warily, as though he expected the hoop to reach out and bite him.

"What's the working time? I mean, as we use time for everyday purposes, how long would it take to arrive back at, say 80,000 years?"

"The tests respond to signals spaced at four seconds."

"Then a man wouldn't have time for much sight-seeing on the way."

"I doubt if he would even be conscious of the mechanical stopovers. He would merely arrive at his destination. That is, if all goes well."

"Hoping again," Doc Tom sighed, although there didn't seem to be any great fear in his reactions. "You said you needed money to —"

"It amounts to this: you would land where I pointed you."

"But you feel you can iron out these bugs, as you call them?"

"I sincerely hope so."

"I do too." Doc Tom stepped onto the platform. "Is this it? Does a man just step through — ?"

"No. Hold it a minute."

Dad pulled one of the switches. Nothing happened. That is, nothing visible. But you could feel a high-tension sing through the room. And I missed the process because I was watching Dad, until I heard Doc Tom exclaim, "Well, I'll be a monkey's stepson." And I looked and saw that the ring had disappeared.

"It's gone!" I bleated.

"No," Dad said, "it's still there. But the vibrations of the metal have reached a point where your eyes can no longer record the form."

"Why, of course!" Doc Tom said. "It's so simple, I should have known."

Dad pulled a second switch and then began adjusting some of the controls on the board. And where the ring had been there now appeared what can be described only as a circular rainbow.

Doc Tom stepped back off the platform. "H'mmm," he said. "No end. Therefore, no pot of gold."

"The pot of gold is somewhere on the other side," Dad said. "At least I hope it is."

"That's what I like about you, Sam," Doc Tom said. "You're so dead certain about everything."

"The mechanism appears to short-circuit time, if that

makes any sense to you. It contracts time, so to speak. Within the dimensions of that circle, time is moving in reverse at an incredible speed. That was the problem: to move time fast enough so that it would have no effect on matter. If it moved slower, the man entering the tunnel's operating range would grow progressively younger as he moved back into earlier time patterns."

"H'mmm," Doc Tom murmured. "You make time move so fast it doesn't have time to —"

Dad was half smiling. "Tom, I always said you were wasting yourself as a paleontologist. You'd make a better comedian. But now, if you don't mind, take the screwdriver off that table and toss it into the ring."

Doc Tom reached for the screwdriver and did as Dad directed. The tool vanished.

"Where did it go?"

"Into the past, I hope."

The dramatic side of it hit me. "Say!" I exclaimed, "right now maybe someone is holding that screwdriver 10,000 years ago and gibbering about magic."

Dad was frowning. "I'm sorry. I didn't use my head. That wasn't a very smart thing to do. I hope the screwdriver isn't buried in some poor unfortunate's chest."

"The odds are way against it," I said.

"Thank heaven for that. Anyhow, this is my brainchild. A little more money and work —"

He had turned off the power, and the ring had reappeared. Doc Tom was moving back toward Dad and the door. "Sam," he asked, "what's the situation with this contraption?"

Dad knew what he meant. "Technically — and ethically

— it belongs to the university, with the Hellman Foundation asserting some control. There's something along those lines in the fine print. The machine is not what we went after in the original research, in that it did nothing to solve the gravity problem — other than perhaps prove we were on the wrong track."

"Then if I shift some of my money —"

"You'll get it back eventually. I'm completely free to continue the work, because it comes under the head of my original research."

"So we're on clear ground."

"Oh yes. My big regret is that I can't be the first man to walk through it. I wouldn't dare trust the controls to anyone else at this stage."

"But, Sam, I know you well enough to know you wouldn't send anyone else through it unless you were positive —"

"As positive as anyone can be about an untried —"

They hadn't noticed that I wasn't with them, and the door closed, cutting off their voices. I stood there alone, staring at the fantastic metal ring. The reason I'd taken no part in the conversation was that I'd been speechless. Both Dad and Doc Tom were basically scientists. Doc Tom, with all his light kidding, was as rock-solid as they came. So neither of them was greatly moved by the sheer romance and adventure of the thing.

But I was. And I stood there trying to contain my excitement. I'd just listened to two men talking calmly and quietly about going back into the past — something that not only had never been done but was considered impos-

sible. On the other side of that ring were all the secrets
mankind had puzzled over from the beginning.

Beyond that ring Napoleon was still fighting the Battle
of Waterloo. On the other side of it was a great stage on
which everything that had ever happened was still hap-
pening.

There, the War of the Roses and the building of the
pyramids would be like yesterday. And the cavemen killing their meat with clubs, only a few months ago.

The age of the dinosaurs! They were still living and
fighting and dying back there!

I had enough common sense to know which way the
weather vane pointed — why Dad had shown his secret
machine to Doc Tom. It hadn't been for the money. He
could have gotten that from several places.

Doc Tom was slated to be the first-time traveler. He was
going back to see his dinos firsthand. Obviously Dad had
thought that a paleontologist would be the ideal man to
make the time trip. And he would know beforehand how
greatly Doc Tom would appreciate the privilege.

Behind their light banter and casual approaches, they
were both practical, hardheaded dreamers, if that term
means anything.

But they'd overlooked someone. Me. Somehow, by hook
or crook, I was going to make that trip too. Doc Tom
wasn't the only one who liked dinos!

Making this firm resolve, I turned out the lights and
ran after them, not wanting to miss anything they might
have to say.

The Rainbow Ring

I HARDLY SLEPT THAT NIGHT; my excitement was at its peak. But things didn't stay that way, and the letdown was terrible.

I came to breakfast the next morning all primed to talk about Dad's great discovery or invention, or whatever he wanted to call it.

He didn't want to call it either one, and wasn't in the least excited about it.

"The time-travel thing, Bob? Oh yes. It's only research, you understand. Something may come of it."

"Something may come of it! Why, Dad, we saw it last night! You've got it made!"

"Oh, good heavens, no! We may hit a stone wall any day now. We have our other research too — the important work —"

"The important work! What could be more important than going back into time?"

"Oh, quite a few things. Finding out exactly what time is, for one thing. Solving the time-space riddle." As usual, he had a magazine propped up in front of his plate and was peering at it over his coffee cup.

"Did you read about the amazing work that was recently done on antibodies? If you're looking for romance in science, that's where you might find it. Imagine a world the exact opposite of ours existing somewhere. It staggers the imagination."

But I wasn't interested in antiworlds. I was interested in time travel, and I badgered Dad into letting me watch the work that he would be doing on the machine in the back room at his laboratory.

And it was pretty dull.

Dad had three assistants. Gabe Rickson was his number one man, and we got along very well together as long as I stayed out of his way. He was in his late fifties and might have been rated as a sourpuss. But when you really knew him, you found this wasn't true. It was only that he had no interest whatever in anything but science, and he didn't want anybody getting in his way — least of all a gawking seventeen-year-old with big feet. But if I kept my feet out of his way, he was quite friendly and at times would actually talk to me.

Lee Sommes, a younger man, dedicated to science and tennis, always had the same question for me: "Why aren't you in school cracking your books, so you can be half the physicist your father is when you're twice his age?"

First, I told Lee this was summer vacation, but that

didn't make any sense to him. Only idiots took vacations. Then I told him I wasn't interested in being a physicist, and that was even worse. Only cretins weren't interested in being physicists.

Dave Wyler was more friendly than Lee Sommes or Gabe Rickson. He was always finding things for me to do — like going over to the university lab to pick up four neutrons packed in ice cubes so they wouldn't melt, or climbing the clock tower after a bagful of wind to test for high-flying mushroom spores. A real comedian, Dave, but a top scientific mind.

I wasn't able to generate excitement in any of them over the astounding possibilities of Dad's time-travel machine.

Lee Sommes said, "The Dinosaur Age? Sure. Great place to get stranded without a subway token."

Dave Wyler was even more cynical: "Ha! You want to go see the dinosaurs. But I'll bet you haven't been to the local zoo in a year. They've got funny-looking animals there too, you know. And you can make the scene for fifteen cents."

Gabe Rickson didn't kid, but he showed me how tough it was. One day they were making a test — throwing a small cotton ball through the ring — and he pointed to a board with twenty-six dials on it and said, "Robert, when every one of those dials reacts by pointing its needle at zero at precisely the same second, we will be close to a real test of the device."

The cotton ball made them point in twenty-six different directions, so to me success seemed almost impossible.

But that was the difference between me and Dad. He and his three able helpers kept on placidly hammering at the impossible until it gave up after long weary days — probably when it decided that bucking these guys just wasn't worthwhile.

So the work had gone on without a hitch, the necessary money passing smoothly from Doc Tom's budgetary allotment over to Dad's.

Then one evening three weeks later Doc Tom came to dinner again, and this time he brought Pete.

Pete was Doc Tom's son, and while I didn't especially like him, that wasn't to say I disliked him. We were just different types. He was a brain — no doubt about that — and I always got the idea he thought of my football and baseball and tennis efforts as a waste of time. The closest he came to athletics was an occasional dip in the pool. But I had to give him credit there. Whatever he did take up, he did well. He could spot me half the length of the pool and beat me every time.

All in all, however, Pete was a nice kid.

So he came along with his dad to dinner that night, and after Grace brought the coffee in, Dad said, "By the way, Tom, that test today was a complete success. It looks as though we're ready."

Evidently they'd had some talks I hadn't been in on, because it all seemed to be arranged. The light mood of the previous dinner was gone too.

"The only possible risk that I see," Dad said, speaking to Doc Tom, "is getting you back. But the risk is reduced to a minimum."

"A small one for the importance of the experiment," Doc Tom said gravely.

"I'd give everything to be able to go myself."

"I know that. But if it were possible, I'd still scramble for the privilege of being first. It's no small honor, you know."

Pete had put down his fork. He was staring at his father. "Dad, what is this?"

He evidently hadn't been told, and I noticed that Doc Tom seemed a little embarrassed. He'd no doubt had his reasons for keeping Pete in the dark, but now he had to face up to it.

"It's an experiment in time travel, son."

Pete's expression hid a lot that was underneath. But it revealed a lot too.

"Is it dangerous?"

Doc Tom laughed. "Why, Pete, crossing the street is dangerous these days."

"But what you're planning is more dangerous than crossing the street."

"A little, perhaps."

"Exactly what is it?"

There was a queer switch here — as though they'd changed places and Pete was the parent. Pete had no mother either, but she wasn't dead. I'd never inquired, although I was sure Dad knew about it. I thought Doc Tom was divorced, but if Pete had been the victim of a broken home, he seemed to have survived it all right. I guess I read his face with that in mind and saw him wondering if he was going to lose his father too.

"Sam has been working on a time-travel problem," Doc Tom said, "and he's come up with a pretty sensational answer."

"By that I guess you mean you're going to try to travel in time?"

Doc Tom tried the light smile, but didn't do very well at it. "I'm going to take a crack at it, Pete."

"Which way? Forward or backward?"

"Backward, of course."

"But why you?"

"There are good reasons. I've been planning to brief you on the operation. I'll give you all the details when we get home."

Pete's questions hadn't been in any way impudent. They'd been very quiet inquiries into something important he hadn't been let in on, and I think his reaction was mixed. He was hurt at having been left out, and he was plenty worried about Doc Tom's safety.

But he was adult about it and said, "O.K., Dad. I'd like to hear."

Another good mark for Pete's character was the way he handled it afterward. With dinner over, he and I went to the rumpus room where we had a table, and we shot some pool. Pete, with a grasp of angular geometry that left me floundering, beat me from here to there. But at no time did he try to pump me or blow his top at having been left out.

Well, that's not quite accurate. After we put up our cues and started to leave the rumpus room, he murmured, "I guess Dad just didn't know how to tell me." But he was talking more to himself than anyone else. I said nothing, but I got the idea he and his father had more difficulty with communication than Dad and I did. And I felt a little sorry for him. . . .

After that, there was no fanfare or any big ceremony. In fact, the whole thing was underplayed. Take-off time, if that was what it could be called, was set for ten forty-five the next morning.

I went to the laboratory with Dad at eight thirty, and before that, during breakfast, neither of us referred to the big thing that was going to happen. We talked about football — what my chances of making all-city next year were — but it was easy to see that neither of us was much interested.

When we got to the lab, I parked myself in a corner out of the way and watched the final check-out. Gabe, Lee, and Dave worked like units in a machine, and for all you could see this was exactly like any other day.

They had a check-out routine that I didn't understand, but I had one thing to watch and go on: the dials and that little ball of cotton.

They finally arrived at that point in the check-out, and when the cotton ball was tossed into the circular rainbow and vanished, it was heartening to see every one of the twenty-six needles jump to zero and stand there as though they'd been frozen.

I turned from watching the dials to look at Dad's face. It told me nothing — gave me no news at all. I had to hope that no news was good news, so I glued my eyes to the dials and then I heard Dad snap, "O.K. — get it back."

Gabe did some manipulating on the control board, and a few seconds later the cotton ball popped out again. It gave me the weird feeling that this had been the objective of Dad's experiment: to build a machine that manufactured little cotton balls and tossed them out, one at a time, on the platform.

Dad's tension was revealed in the way he pounced on the ball and took it to a table where he had a battery of microscopes. He began testing it while his three assistants stood around him.

After a while he straightened up. "No damage," he announced.

I thought I heard a collective sigh go up.

"It looks as though the grounding gradient potential works," Gabe muttered. The relief in his voice was so great that it had the reverse effect. It sounded as though he were grumbling at the perfection achieved.

"It does seem to be adjusted correctly," Dad said.

I stood there with half my mind on what they were doing and the other half of it on my own plans. In this last half I visualized myself moving with perfect timing — stepping ahead of Doc Tom at the right moment and walking casually through the round rainbow. That was what I'd been planning. I knew I'd have to face Dad afterward, but there would be one good thing about it: the relief to Pete when I blocked Doc Tom out of the dangerous experiment.

Of course, I dreaded the session with Dad later, but I figured it this way: If I didn't come back, there wouldn't be any problem. And if I did, the success of the experiment would take the sting out of facing him.

At least I hoped it would.

"So it's set," Lee Sommes said as he turned away from the table. He could have been saying the coffee was ready as far as his tone of voice was concerned. But he wasn't fooling anybody. Underplaying the thing only heightened the tension in the lab.

Then the air was tightened even more by the arrival of Doc Tom and Pete. Evidently, they'd had their talk, and Pete was reconciled to his father's going. He was silent and completely in control of himself, but his pallor and the redness of his eyes showed he hadn't done any sleeping the night before.

There was one comedy aspect to the thing, but it wasn't funny, only grotesque: the way Doc Tom was dressed. He wore heavy, knee-high boots and thick corduroy pants. Thick leather gauntlets and a woolen cap with earflaps completed his costume. He had a pack on his back and a camera slung over one shoulder. There was a .45 automatic holstered on one hip and a hunting knife on the other, and he carried a rifle that could have knocked a rhino over.

Pete came over and stood beside me out of the way and we watched the final preparations.

Dad said, "All right, Tom. I've set the unit for fourteen jumps — as far as I dare. The safety factors check out, but the power capacity —"

Doc Tom nodded. "If you say so, I'll settle for that."

Then Pete surprised me. "That's eighty million years," he said in a whisper.

There was dissatisfaction in Doc Tom's voice, and Pete went on to explain: "They disputed that point. Your father wanted a minimum hop in the shortest possible time. That would have been 10,000 years."

"That seems logical," I answered, but only to have something to say. I had my own problems. I was wrestling with the thought of landing eighty million years back in my shirt sleeves, because that was how I was dressed. I was also watching things in order to gauge my own timing — to reach the ring at just the right moment so that they wouldn't be able to stop me.

"But Dad insisted on an all-out test," Pete was saying. "All the way. Your father finally gave in."

I felt sorry for Pete, but I admired him at the same time. As far as he knew for sure, he was standing in at his father's execution. In a way, it was no different than if he'd been watching Doc Tom being strapped into the electric chair.

And it wasn't just Doc Tom. It was his father.

Now Dad made a final rundown check of the board and turned toward the platform. There was no melodrama, no handshaking or shoulder-slapping or well-good-luck-old-chap business. The thing was kept rigidly in the realm of a scientific research with the human element removed.

This confused me and threw me off balance. I hadn't expected it to work that way. I thought there would be a little emotion displayed before Doc Tom stepped back into the unknown — a chance for me to stand on the platform and shake his hand and get in front of him for my big play.

But what really happened was that on signal from Dad, Gabe started a ten-second clock on the panel and Dad said, "O.K., position," and Doc Tom moved forward and stood in front of the rainbow ring.

I took a step toward the platform, and without even looking in my direction, Dad snapped, "Stay where you are."

I froze.

"Walk through," Dad said, and at the very last moment Doc Tom smiled and raised his hand toward Pete. Pete's hand had been on my shoulder, and I felt his nails bite in as he raised his other hand in an answering salute.

Then Doc Tom stepped through the ring and disappeared just like the little cotton ball. And I was left standing in the corner.

So much for my big grandstand play. Of course Dad had stopped me. I had this alibi to play around with, but it didn't help much. It was too lame to stand up, because even if Dad hadn't barked at me, I would still have been a long way from the platform where the action was.

I not only felt like an idiot, but I realized I'd actually been one for thinking I could have gotten away with such a harebrained scheme.

The aftermath was pure letdown. The thing had been done. Doc Tom had stepped into the rainbow ring and disappeared, and we all stood there looking at one another.

And I learned something. There's no feeling on earth so futile and helpless as the one that hits scientists when an experiment has passed the point of no return — especially one in which human life is at stake.

Dad and his three assistants were watching the signal board, and I knew exactly what was going through their minds. They were thinking of all the things that could go wrong; that maybe the whole idea was wrong in the first place; that they could have overlooked some vital factor that would show up at any moment and they'd have to say, "Why didn't we think of that?"

It has to be that way during the big wait when the men have nothing to do *but* worry.

"The board looks good," Dad said.

Pete and I had come forward now, there being no objections, and we stood behind them as they checked the dials. From where I stood, I could see Gabe's face. He was frowning.

"I don't like the power register," he said.

I followed his eyes up to the top of the board along with everyone else and saw the needle holding like iron, and wondered what he didn't like about it. The registration looked perfect to me.

But Dad looked at the dial and then glanced sharply at Gabe and began checking the board again. And I could tell that he depended more on Gabe's instinct than the dial needles.

"Overmassed?" Dad asked.

"Could be. Weight. Displacement. Or both."

"The board's holding steady."

"Too steady. You know what my idea was on that."

"You wanted to see some wavering in light-speed control."

"It seemed to me a variable should show up there. But it doesn't."

"It doesn't have to," Dave Wyler said loyally. But Dad paid no attention to him. He still spoke to Gabe.

"Can we compensate?"

Dad was asking Gabe's opinion on compensation, whatever that was, and he would make his decision after balancing his own opinion with Gabe's.

"It's a guess," Gabe said. "That's our blind spot."

"It might lock him out."

"It could. The computer gave us no alternative."

"The percentages say leave it," Dad replied.

"Right."

This was no place for sentiment, but I wondered if they realized what they were doing to Pete. Standing there scientifically debating his father's welfare.

Pete, however, took it well. He turned away from the board, and I walked with him to the far side of the lab where we leaned against a table, and Pete said, "He's due back in half an hour, our time."

One thing was certain. Maybe Doc Tom had been slow in briefing Pete, but when he did, he'd given him the whole picture.

Pete said, "If the test goes wrong, it won't be your father's fault. What they're talking about, weight and displacement, wouldn't have been a problem in the one hop that your father wanted. Dad wanted the whole eighteen, the unit's capacity."

Pete wore glasses with big round lenses, and when I looked at him I saw the whole board reflected in each of them. Behind them his eyes held steady on the board, and I got the idea he was reading it with as much knowledge as Dad and the other three.

"What is weight and displacement?" I asked.

"Dad said it was the difference between the size and weight of a small ball of cotton and a human body. That simplifies it. But it has something to do with the bending of the light rays going around a small or larger object and the frictional weight drag involved."

"He'll come back O.K.," I said.

28

"Of course," Pete said.

But the half-hour passed. Dad set the machine for the return. As the crucial seconds dragged by, Pete said, "The ring is re-formed at the far time end and holds for twenty-eight seconds. It can be damaged at that end — jammed — and the entrance time can pass. If that happens, Dad can enter on the next cycle."

It was a minute and ten seconds after the half-hour.

"That's probably what happened," I said.

"I hope so."

At the board, Dad spoke with a casualness that was a dead giveaway. "Tom was delayed. He'll catch the next cycle."

And Peter showed a bravery I admired as he said, "He probably got interested in some rocks or something and missed the time."

"Sure," Gabe said, "after all, he is a paleontologist."

"Next cycle," Lee Sommes said carelessly. But there was nothing careless in the way he kept his eyes glued to the dials.

The next cycle came.

It passed.

Doc Tom did not step out of the rainbow ring.

The next.

And the next.

Finally, six hours later, Gabe spoke grimly. "We've got to close it down. The main power tube is ready to go."

"O.K.," Dad said. "Shut it down."

Something had happened. Experiment finished. Result negative.

Doc Tom was gone.

Hard Decision

I ASKED PETE TO STAY at our place that night, and he
seemed glad to. Dad wasn't there. He and his crew went
into a long shift — all night and well into the next day —
working on the power unit of the machine.

Pete didn't want to talk about what had happened, and
I could see why. With him being a brain, I didn't suggest
going out to get a Coke or a malted or anything like that.
I asked if he'd like to play a game of chess, and he said he
would.

It was a weird game for me because I wasn't used to silence. I wasn't even used to chess, for that matter, and
after we'd sat there for half an hour I decided to speak
my mind.

"Somebody's got to go after your father," I said.

Pete sat back and looked at me through those big lenses. "At least we know where he went: to the far end of the time span."

"I don't think anything went wrong with the machine except the strain on the power after they kept it going too long."

"I agree," Pete said. "I won't admit that mechanical failure destroyed Dad. There are too many other possibilities."

"They admit the tunnel could be jammed at the other end."

"And it's only common sense that Dad could have run into trouble when he stepped out into the Dinosaur Age."

I didn't build on that — that Doc Tom could have stepped smack into death by some kind of violence at that end. I knew the idea was high on Pete's list of possibilities.

"I've got to know what happened to him," Pete said.

"You're not going alone. I'm going with you."

Pete gave me a long, level look and was slow about answering. Then he said, "I'd like to have you come, Bob. I know myself pretty well, and I'm not too strong in the physical department. You're a natural athlete."

"And you're plenty cerebral. That counts for more. Any stupe with brawn can run through a football line."

"I've stayed away from sports because I'm physically timid," he said. "I wouldn't admit that under any circumstances other than these. But I think it's important that we understand each other."

"I think we'd make a pretty good team." I grinned, hoping to cheer him up a little. "You could be the quarterback and call the signals. I'll carry the ball in the running game."

His face remained dead serious. "I think we ought to consider it more on an equal basis. We'll both be sharing the physical dangers, so we'll make our decisions together."

"There's only one problem."

"What's that?"

"Dad. *We've* decided to go and look for your father. But what's Sam Miller, head of the operation, going to say?"

Dad said it fifteen minutes later when we went to the laboratory and told him what *we'd* decided.

"Nonsense," he said. "I'm going myself as soon as we make a few more checks."

Pete opened his mouth to protest, but Dad went on. "Pete, I realize how you feel. You want to do something to help. Doing nothing is maddening under circumstances like these. But the responsibility is mine. I allowed your father to take the longer jump against my better judgment, and the risk involved in going after him is mine alone."

"But, sir, doesn't the same point hold as before?"

"What point?"

"You have to stay here to handle the machine."

Gabe looked up from the sheet of figures he was studying. He wasn't a young man, and the strain and long hours were telling. His face was pale and drawn.

"It's still true, Sam."

"Nonsense," Dad repeated brusquely. "You can handle things as well as I can. Your instincts are better than mine."

Gabe straightened as the other two men watched silently. He rubbed his back. "It's not quite as simple as that. I'm a number two man, Sam, and I always will be. If I wasn't, I'd have been number one somewhere long ago."

"But, Gabe —"

"You know the limitations of the second-level man. He's good under supervision. He's very courageous and daring in his decisions as long as he knows the number one man will countermand him or take the responsibility. That's why a lot of first mates never rise to be captains."

"But there would be nothing to it now. We've proved that the gradient adjustment was right and that the space-time factor did not intrude —"

Pete's face lighted up. "Then even without conclusive data, you —"

Dad waved a quick hand. "That isn't the point. I'm not going to let a seventeen-year-old boy —"

"Two seventeen-year-old boys, Dad," I cut in. "That makes thirty-four years' experience —"

"Absolutely not!"

"Then start looking for a time traveler, Sam. I won't take the responsibility at this end."

Anger flashed in Dad's eyes, but it faded quickly as he looked at Gabe Rickson.

"I'm sorry, Sam," Gabe said.

"It's all right. I understand. If I insisted, I'd be forcing you to take the brunt of my original mistake. That's the trouble with making the prime error. Other errors automatically stem from it."

"But you can't blame yourself, Dr. Miller," Pete said. "You've proven against a flaw in the machine. Therefore,

Dad ran into trouble at the far end. So it was eighty million years. There would just as easily have been equal danger at the 10,000-year level."

"That's true, Sam," Dave Wyler said. "You can't blame yourself."

Dad evaded by saying, "It really doesn't matter now. The point is, we've got to get to Tom as soon as we can."

"That's right," Pete said, "there's no time for you to hunt up another man, brief him on the operation, and trust him with it. It would take time to find the right one."

"He's got a point," Lee Sommes said. "Look, Sam — let me take a crack at it."

"Impossible."

I wondered about that. In fact, I'd figured from the start that one of the three men would try to move in ahead of us, and I wondered why it had taken so long for at least one of them to offer.

I found out later. It was physical condition. Lee was under forty, but he had a prohibitive heart condition. Dave Wyler, in his mid-fifties, had already suffered one stroke. And Gabe Rickson's general health was too far off par — too much work under too strenuous conditions.

"Sir," Pete said, "with all due respect, I've got a right to go and help my father."

The pressure was pushing hard on Dad. He made a gesture of brushing everyone aside. "Nothing can be done for three hours, anyhow. That recharging has to be done. Leave me alone. Let me think."

We watched as he strode out of the laboratory, and it was a perfect example of what the head man has to take on his shoulders.

"I'll be back in a little while," he said over his shoulder. Then the door closed behind him.

There was silence for a while, no one having anything to say. Then Gabe began talking, mainly to fill the void, I thought.

"The fault we suspected wasn't there," he said. "Thank heaven it wasn't. The variation we had a right to expect was being lost in a faulty stabilizer platform, but it took time and power to find it. That's why we have to wait now to build up the power."

"How about the other factor? Are you sure my father didn't land ten feet underground or deep underwater?"

"It would have been impossible."

"Some natural hazard may have put him in trouble."

Gabe looked at Pete and spoke quietly. "I know how you feel. You consider it your right to go and help your father. And if my opinion is any comfort, I think Sam will see it your way."

That made me jump, and turned me to thinking about my own interests. If Dad trusted Gabe's instincts, who was I to ignore them?

"I'll be back in a minute," I said, and went hunting for Dad.

I found him at home in his room. I knocked, and there was no answer. Soon there was a quiet, "Come in," and I opened the door and saw him standing by the window looking out but not seeing anything.

He jerked his head around almost angrily, then caught himself. "Yes, Bob?"

"May I speak to you for a moment, sir?"

"Yes."

"I know it's a big decision you have to make."

"You do?"

"Yes, sir," I replied. "I know how we look from where you sit. I know you see us as a couple of kids, but —"

"We? Us?"

"Yes, sir. That's what I wanted to speak to you about. If you let Pete go, you have to let me go with him."

Before he could cut in, I rushed on. "This thing has come down to elementals. Sentiment hasn't got much to do with it. And you've got to admit that you can't send Doc Tom's son to look for him and not send me along."

"Why can't I?"

"Because it would look cowardly — as though you were willing to risk Doc Tom's son, but not your own."

Dad could explode when the occasion demanded, and this could have been a real occasion. I didn't want him to explode, because I knew I'd be better off to let him think about it. So I said, "I just wanted to put that point to you, sir, and now that I've made it I'll be on my way."

I went out the door and closed it quickly after me and rushed downstairs. As I went back to the laboratory I glanced up and saw him still standing by the window. And I was willing to bet he still wasn't seeing anything.

I went back to the laboratory, and with nothing else to do, stood around helping them wait.

And it was no easy job for any of us. . . .

Dad came back an hour later. He'd made his decision. His crisis was over. He was quiet, posed, almost casual.

"I think," he said, "you better go through the ring and see what's keeping Tom. There'll be a few preparations to be made. You'd better get to it."

I almost jumped up and kicked the ceiling. Almost. But instead I took my cue from Pete, who showed no reaction whatever. Pete said, "Thank you, sir. I'm sure we'll find him tied up in some minor difficulty."

"Thanks, Dad," I echoed just as quietly. "Maybe we'd better get some equipment together."

"Do that. I'm going back to the house for a little while. Dave will see that you're outfitted."

I wanted to follow him and thank him again, and tell him how much it meant to me. But I knew he wouldn't have wanted me to. He already knew.

I thought of that. Then all I could think of was the excitement of it.

I was going back into time!

Back to the age of the dinosaurs! . . .

The Big Lizard

THERE WASN'T ANYTHING TO IT. We just stepped through. Perhaps there was a little physical reaction that would have hit a person not in good condition. With me, it was a slight chill. Goose pimples. But that could have been emotional.

Nothing at all.

We stepped into the ring and took one step, and the scene changed. That was it. We were outdoors. The sun was shining and there was a breeze blowing, and my first thought was, "We haven't gone anywhere. We can't see them, but they're still here" — Dad, standing at the edge of the platform hiding everything behind a wall he'd built for the occasion; Gabe, and Lee, and Dave at the control board.

I looked at Pete and said, "We didn't go anywhere."

38

There was a tight smile on his face, and I guess he'd gotten the same sensation, because he said, "I get what you mean, but I don't think it's quite that way."

I didn't either, really. But I couldn't put it into words.

Pete's doubts, however, had a practical basis. As our eyes circled our new surroundings, Pete said, "I never discussed it with your father, but I'm sure there must have been some slippage."

"Some what?"

"It's a word I coined myself to define something I don't quite understand. But coming through time, it seems to me, must be the same as firing a rocket. You can't hit the dime with a shot. You can't orbit a satellite and bring it back to an acre-sized target."

"Slippage," I muttered. I thought it was a good word.

"Eighty million years of time. The galaxy moved. The system moved; the planets moved. We got here, but if we're on the exact spot we started from, it would be a miracle."

"I'm sure that occurred to Dad."

"Of course. But I'm sure he would admit that he couldn't know — even with everything computed — that we would hit dead center."

"Then Doc Tom may not even be around here."

"I figure anywhere within a mile would be practically pinpoint."

"Well, he certainly isn't in sight."

The rainbow ring had stayed with us about ten seconds and had then faded. We were standing in a small grassy park with trees and forest in one direction and rough, bare, rocky country in the other. Kind of on the border line between the two.

Off to our left was a big swamp that went for a mile or so and vanished into the green of the forest. We'd been taking everything in as fast as we could, our rather abstract talk being in the nature of — well, kind of whistling in the graveyard, if you get what I mean.

Were you ever with somebody, and you were both scared of something but neither of you wanted to talk about it? That's the way it was with Pete and me.

We were both scared.

"Our hope is that there's a pattern to it," Pete said.

"What do you mean by that?"

"It's not important at the moment. The thing to do now is try to find Dad."

"That's right, but suppose the slippage is, say, a hundred miles. That wouldn't be much for eighty million years. It would still be practically on the dime."

"Let's just hope it isn't."

"And when the ring comes back —"

"I see no problem there unless some of the basics were wrong," Pete said. "The time-distance isn't important."

I had him! He'd contradicted himself, and that made me happy, so I guess maybe I was a little jealous of Pete — annoyed that his thinking was more orderly and systematic than mine.

"I was referring to how far from the laboratory we've landed," I said. "Your slippage would come to bear on that. But it wouldn't bear on the three days between Doc Tom's trip and ours."

"I think it would, to some extent. So far as the eighty-million-year time span is concerned, we might be standing on a spot in South Africa — or any other place on the globe."

"Then how come we missed landing in the ocean?"

Pete frowned. "You didn't listen very closely. Your father explained that. If he hadn't been able to solve that problem, we couldn't have come in the first place."

I scowled back at him. We might, I thought, just have a little trouble. But he went on before I could say anything.

"The long-term slippage could be anything. The other — let's call it the short-term slippage — could be a hundred yards or a mile or a hundred miles. We won't know until we get some data to go by."

I decided not to argue. His logic was too good. "This jacket is hot," I said, and took it off.

We had the same equipment as Doc Tom's, except for the camera. That hadn't seemed necessary on the rescue mission.

Another very important point had been outlined by Dad before we left.

"We'll reactivate the tunnel every twenty-four hours at the outside," he'd said. "Oftener if we can. It will depend on the power element. The mechanism uses far more than we anticipated. But the twenty-four-hour maximum span we'll guarantee. Also, as a maximum, we can give you twenty-five seconds to get through it. . . ."

"So we've got to be on this spot in exactly twenty-four hours," Pete said, "but there's no guarantee that we'll be going back then. The slippage may move the ring too far away for us to reach in time."

41

"You've got a point," I muttered.

"I'm just hoping there's a pattern to the slippage. And I'll bet your father is too."

"Why leave me out? I'm real full of hope."

Pete smiled and went on. "If there's a pattern and we're close enough to see its second arrival from this spot, then we can plot a course and figure out exactly where to be waiting for the next arrival —" he grinned — "I hope."

The tension had loosened and I laughed. "You're beginning to sound like Dad."

Neither of us would have admitted there'd been any initial fright or wariness; still we both knew there had been. Otherwise why had we arrived back eighty million years with our holsters open and our hands on our gun butts?

But this fright had now diminished, and we were both breathing easier. Pete squinted up at the blazing sun as he took off his jacket.

"Do things look any different to you?"

"Bigger, maybe. Hotter."

"There can't really be much change in only eighty million years."

That sounded odd to me. "My! How we do kick large chunks of time around. Eighty million years. Time for three or four push-ups."

"In the broader sense, that's about all it is."

I was pulling off my pack. "Well, what do we do now?"

To some extent, I suppose, this question tended to acknowledge Pete's leadership of the expedition. I thought of that, but I told myself that as long as Doc Tom was his father, he at least ought to be consulted on our moves.

He was swinging in a circle, covering the landscape. Then he curved his palms around his mouth and let out a yell.

"Dad! Hey! Dad!"

We waited. There was only silence.

"You try."

I cupped my hands and took a deep breath and began to yell. "Testing! Testing! One — two — three — four! Hello! Halloo — hallooo — halllooooo!"

I brought back some echoes, but that was all — faraway, eerie sounds coming back from what seemed a dead world. And I got a creepy feeling that somehow we'd gone backstage — that the scenery had been made and erected, and at any time the actors would soon be along and the drama would start. We'd just gotten here too soon and would have to wait awhile.

"If we can find Dad within the next twenty-four hours," Pete said, "we can begin plotting our chart on the tunnel. We'd have two points to work from."

"Well, we won't win anything standing; obviously your dad isn't within earshot. So which will it be: the forest or the desert?"

"I think it would be smart to find a high point and make a survey, and figure from there."

Pete's manner was quite matter-of-fact, but behind his eyes I could see the fear — fear of the question neither of us would even refer to, let alone ask:

Was Doc Tom still alive?

"O.K.," I said. "Let's try those high rocks over there."

This was wrong. I'd hardly gotten the words out before both of us were racing toward the shelter of the forest.

It was one of those run-first-and-look-afterward situations. We'd been on level ground, all right, but it had turned out to be close to the edge of a bluff on the desert side, because all of a sudden a head as big as a small station wagon came up over the edge. It came higher and higher and higher, and a pair of short arms appeared — or forefeet — or something.

Anyhow, that terrible head kept rearing higher and higher. We could see the long, open maw and rows of teeth like sharpened six-inch spikes.

A prehistoric!

It had two eyes, one on each side. It looked at us through one of them and then turned its head to look at us with the other.

I got a flash of its expression before I was able to make my legs start moving, and while the thing was horrible its look was shaped into a question, as though it were asking, "Well, glory be! Where did you two come from?"

But we were more concerned with where we were going. Into the woods.

"What — is it? I gasped as our feet pounded the ground.

"Tyrannosaurus Rex!" Pete gasped. "You've seen them in the library."

"I wish that one was in the library," I grunted and wondered why it took so long to get to the trees with our traveling at least fifty miles an hour.

"Does it — eat people?"

"It does. Shut up and run."

The ground shook under us, and I knew without looking

that Rex had climbed up on our lawn and was probably already taking out after us.

Then Pete yelled, "Not the trees — this way!" and veered to the right."

"Why not the woods?"

"No protection. He could come in there and trample us."

Pete had spotted a pile of boulders, and that was where we were headed. We got there and found we were in luck. Some of them were ten and fifteen feet across and were heaped loosely enough so that we could crawl in among them.

We wormed into a little rock-buttressed cave, and when we got enough breath back to use some of our strength for other things, we propped our chins on the edge and looked out.

There he stood in all his fearless kingship. A pretty flowery way of putting it, maybe, but that was how he struck me. I took it for granted that he was a *he*, but that really made no difference. He stood erect on three points: his two thick legs and his tail. And with those two useless little arms hanging down, he looked both regal and ridiculous.

My idea about his expression had been an illusion. I could see him full face now as he stood where we'd lately been standing. He had wicked little eyes, and they were looking things over and not liking what they saw. A couple of chunks of dinner had been there when he'd looked over the edge and now they had disappeared.

Rex let out a kind of disgusted bellowing grunt that rattled our eardrums. Maybe he was saying, "O.K., you two, come out and fight like men," in tyranno language. But we weren't accepting any challenges.

Pete stared as though hypnotized. Then he got a little flowery too. "King of the Tyrant Lizards," he muttered.

"King of the what?"

"That's what Tyrannosaurus Rex means," he said.

"I can think of some good names for him too, but I don't use such language."

"I don't think he even saw us."

"You mean he's just taking a walk?"

"Foraging for food, I imagine."

"And he can't see it when it's right under his nose?"

"He probably didn't see very well."

Pete had used the past tense, and that struck me. Maybe because I felt the same way. I couldn't associate with this time and place. I was seeing this twenty-foot-high beast, but I still wasn't believing him somehow.

"One thing," Pete said. "He tells us where we are."

"Where?"

"In the Mesozoic era. It had three periods, you know."

"Oh, sure. They're on the tip of my tongue, but —"

"The Triassic, the Jurassic, and the Cretaceous."

"That's just what I was about to say."

"It covered about a hundred and thirty million years."

"Correction. *Is going to,* you mean. We're in it. We're with it. We're on the scene — remember?"

"It's awfully hard to get used to."

"I'm with you on that."

"I'd say we're somewhere in the Cretaceous. You may see things that will haunt your dreams."

"I won't be surprised at anything I see — after *that.*"

We hadn't taken our eyes off our buck-toothed friend. He was peering around in hostile fashion, his grunts a small blast furnace coughing up hot steel. He seemed to be saying he could trounce anybody in the coffee shop, and where was everybody.

"He's why it was so quiet when we got here," Pete said. "The rest of the animal population heard him coming and left."

"They're a lot smarter than we were. How long do you suppose he'll keep us penned up?"

"He'll probably move on shortly."

But then our interest was drawn elsewhere. Our rocks, and everything else around us, began to shake.

"Earthquake," I bleated.

"Volcano," Pete said. And he was correct. There was a sound like far-off thunder, and straight ahead of us, over the harsh, rocky desert, a great spout of black smoke smeared up into the sky. The earth continued to shake and the black smoke billowed, and then, close to the horizon, it was riding a cushion of red fire.

"A big one," Pete muttered. "I hope it doesn't break things up."

I remembered now that the age of the dinosaurs was also the age of the volcanos. Fire spouts dotted the land, and the earth was a great round furnace with safety valves close to the surface.

Rex turned and looked at the spouting volcano and challenged it to a fight. When he got no action, he sneered at it from deep in his throat and started toward the woods.

The volcano had merely burped a little, grumbling over an upset stomach, and now the vibration of the earth, less violent, was caused by Rex's feet as he lumbered past us.

He crashed into the forest like five trailer trucks hitting the trees in a single crash. Something arose out of the forest with a horrible squawk — a hideous-looking flying nightmare of a bird. It had no feathers, only an oily-looking, dark-brown skin, and didn't appear to have much flesh on it — like a skeleton framework with ghoulish skin stretched over it. The flying monstrosity had an ugly beak at least two feet long.

We heard Rex bellow out a contemptuous challenge — one the bird declined to accept. Then it flapped off toward the desert, its wings creaking over our heads.

"One of the Pterodactyl family. A Pteranodon, maybe. Some of them had wingspreads of over twenty feet," Pete said.

I blinked and had to recall that he was a paleontologist's son. Everyone to his own talent. I was handicapped because there were no great football players loping by. Had there been, I could have named them and casually mentioned each one's complete background.

But this seemed hardly a place for competition. The sun was moving toward what I confidently supposed was the west, and we'd laid out no campaign whatever.

We climbed out of our cubbyhole and I asked, "We'd better start hunting for your father, hadn't we? Or else try to find a safe place to bed down for the night. And how about some food?"

We'd brought enough high-protein stuff for two or three meals, but moving much food through the tunnel hadn't been practicable. We were supposed to live off the land. I thought of this, but I told myself that if it came down to chewing on one of the drumsticks I'd seen flying over our heads, I wasn't going to do much eating.

"The tyranno seems to have moved on," Pete said, "so let's try the forest."

"O.K., but let's be careful."

One thing — Pete didn't resent some of the cracks I made. He understood that my cynical front was only a peg to hang my courage on. And because my courage was pretty limp, I needed a stout peg.

"Let's go," he said.

We got into the woods easily because our big-footed zoological specimen had broken quite an opening for us. And he'd cleared away a lot of what could have been dangerous animal life.

The temperature dropped sharply as we went into the shade. The ground underneath was damp and quite solid. Most of it was impassable unless we followed the path of the great beast that had forced its way through. The tyranno had broken down all the smaller trees in its path, and many bright-colored tendrils and vines and creeping parasites were strung out along its path like long, bright ribbons.

"Watch out for snakes," Pete said, "although I imagine most of them will be over near the swamp."

I stopped suddenly. "Look, this doesn't make sense, our slogging around in here."

He asked why silently, with his eyes, and I said, "First, the tunnel will come out on open ground when it comes. And second, Doc Tom will be expecting help. He'll be looking for us as hard as we're looking for him."

"So —?"

"He'll stay in the open. And he'll expect us to do the same thing."

"That makes sense."

I was pretty proud of myself. I'd come up with something Pete had to approve of.

Pete said, "Then we'd better — *Look out!*"

I saw pure horror wash into his face and turned to look where he was looking, over my shoulder, and saw a multicolored nightmare slithering silently toward us.

Nightmare from the Sea

AT FIRST IT LOOKED like a human face — a hideously evil old man with a jawful of terrible teeth lunging toward us through the heavy growth. This old man had a stringy beard of many colors that streamed out behind the great savage head.

Then I saw the long, twisting body behind it. It was a garishly colored sea serpent of incredible length. We had warning because the great reptile was approaching along the path broken by the Tyrannosaurus. If this had not been the case, it could have been upon us from cover and we would not have had a chance.

We had our rifles, and though it had made no sense to

use them on the tyranno, this was a different situation. I brought mine up and fired. Of course I missed. Hitting the twisting, slithering thing would have been a miracle.

Pete stood frozen, staring at the monstrosity, his eyes fixed as if he'd gone under hypnosis.

"Run!" I yelled. "Try to make open land. There's no protection in here."

All we could have done in that jungle growth would have been to get tangled in undergrowth and become easy prey.

I fired once more and turned to run. Sudden fright had distorted the picture a little, and I'd seen the monster reptile as coming with the speed of the wind.

But this was not the case. A lot of its swift movement was an illusion produced by the winding movement of its long, foot-thick body and the odd way it had of thrusting its head eight or ten feet forward and then jerking it back as it moved.

"Run!" I yelled again, and in desperation I slapped Pete's ashen face.

This brought him out of it, and we were both kiting back to where we'd come from, with that horrible hissing sound coming right along behind us.

The snake was gaining ground, but not as fast as I'd feared it would. The hissing, like the continuous escape of hot, angry steam, grew louder. But the edge of the forest was close.

We dashed out into the open, and now Pete got his voice back. "This is crazy! Out here it's sure to get us."

"It was sure to get us in there. Out here we can fight, but I've got a hunch about something. Follow me."

The reptile had hesitated at the edge of the forest and I glanced back and saw it more clearly. It was even more hideous than it had appeared in the jungle, but now I saw that its frightful beard was a lot of the creepers and tendrils the tyranno had torn loose. The snake had hooked onto them like long confetti as it came through.

I pointed out the way toward some rough, scaly ground I'd seen beside the rock pile where we'd hidden from the big lizard, and as I kept glancing back at the snake I saw that it was hesitating because it was unsure of its ground.

The head stood on six or seven feet of its erect length; the rest of its thirty- or forty-foot body was used to wind along the ground and give it locomotion. As I watched, running sideways, the snake began hissing louder and moved the front part of itself back and forth along the edge of the grass, a cross-movement covering perhaps ten feet, as though it hunted a place to push through onto the new surface.

That gave me hope that my idea might work out. When the snake made the plunge into the grass and came forward again, I faced around and caught up with Pete.

I debated stopping to take my chances with my rifle and pistol, but decided against it. If my idea fizzled out, there would still be time for that in a last stand.

"That way," I yelled. "Into that rough stuff."

Ahead of us was about two acres of level ground covered with coarse gravel and small bits of boulder that would have sliced our feet to ribbons in five steps if we'd been barefoot.

Of course we had heavy boots on, but even then we stepped carefully once we'd entered the field because some of the larger boulder scraps could have sliced through the leather covering our ankles.

"Straight in," I said. "Over to the other side."

We'd come close to the far edge when the snake, clearly planning to have us for dinner, reached the field. We stopped and waited.

"Get out your .45," I said. "If it comes through, wait till it's fifty feet away and then blast for the head."

"And hope we can hit it," Pete muttered.

"Also that slugs will stop it if we do hit it."

The snake was closer to us now than it had been at the forest edge and was probably hungrier. That made it less cautious, and it slivered onto the rock field.

But then it hissed horribly and stopped and pulled back.

"What's wrong with it?" Pete said. "Why doesn't it come on?"

"I hope it's because the rocks cut its belly. There's deep water around here somewhere. That's a sea serpent —"

"But this is the wrong age," Pete wailed. "They've all died off."

"O.K.," I said grimly, "just yell out and tell Buster over there it doesn't exist. Maybe it'll be confused and leave."

Pete was gripping the butt of his .45. "Why not try a few shots? Maybe we'll get lucky and stop the thing."

"I think maybe it's stopped now. I hope so. If we hit it and hurt it, it might get mad enough to come through the rocks, regardless."

The serpent was hissing horribly. It tried the rocks again, but they weren't the same as the soft, muddy bottoms of the sea and the marshes, and its belly wasn't conditioned.

But the snake had an intelligence of a sort. This showed when it began coming around the rock patch to get at us from the other side. But when it got to our side, we were on the other.

"This can go on all night," Pete said.

"Let's try a few shots then," I said. "If we stay out here much longer, one of those flying skeletons may come along and we really will be in trouble."

"You go ahead," Pete said. "You're a better shot than I am."

I shouldered my rifle and centered on the huge head, moving with it, waiting for a still moment. The head moved back and forth horizontally. Then, when the rifle was beginning to get pretty heavy, the snake had a motionless moment.

I pressed the trigger. And I was lucky. I didn't kill the thing, but I scored a hit that brought out the grandaddy of all hissing screams, and the reptile began thrashing wildly.

It had been hurt; some instinct for its native habitat asserted itself, and it headed back for the trees. We both sighed weakly as it disappeared beyond the green wall.

We picked our way out of the field and sat down on one of the boulders.

"What do we do now?" I said.

Pete was silent. Not getting an answer, I glanced his way. His shoulders were bent, and he hung his head dejectedly.

"You take over, Bob."

"What do you mean?"

"I chickened out under pressure. I froze back there in

the woods. You saved both our lives. If it hadn't been for you, I'd be in that snake's belly by now."

"You're off your crock! Besides, this isn't a leader-follower deal. We're not a squad of soldiers. We're two guys trying to get along, and each of us needs what the other's got. You can save my life tomorrow."

Pete tried to grin. "If we live that long."

"We will. What's your idea about a fire and some hot food?"

"What hot food? We've got nothing to cook."

"You're right. We're supposed to live off the land. But so far, I haven't seen anything very appetizing."

Pete was frowning. "About the fire — I don't know. It's supposed to keep wild animals at bay. At least it does in our own age. But here —"

"What do you mean?"

"These animals have very small brains. Maybe memory patterns haven't developed. They might fear fire only when it burns them."

"It's a point," I said.

"So maybe a fire would just bring a lot of them to investigate."

"I guess we'd better just hole up in these rocks for the night."

"We could probably block ourselves in with small boulders. That would leave only one risk."

"What's that?"

"Snakes. But I haven't seen any."

Pete shuddered. "I have."

"I mean rock snakes. Dry land reptiles."

"There may be lizards."

"We'll have to gamble on that."

"O.K. Let's eat."

We opened a can of meat and ate it with biscuits out of an airtight bag. It tasted great. We'd brought water too, of course, and when we allowed ourselves two rations, we felt a lot better.

The sun was winging down over the marsh, approaching the horizon.

"There's ocean over there somewhere," I said.

"Close, too," Pete answered.

"This is an odd spot we hit. Ocean, marsh, and forest on one side — desert on the other."

"Let's locate a night spot before it gets too dark."

We inspected the big rock pile and finally settled for a protected ledge up high.

Pete got up there first and cried, "Hey, you can see the ocean from here."

I climbed up beside him and there it was, off beyond the marsh, a vast, endless expanse of mysterious water. We stared in silence. Then Pete asked, "Does it look different to you?" He spoke in a kind of hushed voice.

"Different?"

"Uh-huh. It sure is ocean and it sticks to the land and goes to the horizon just like oceans are supposed to do. But —"

"I get what you mean. Out there with the swamp on the side of it and the green forest off to the left, it's — well, kind of eerie."

"Like — like a world waiting to be born."

I grinned. "Why, Pete, I didn't know you were the poetic type."

But still I knew what he meant. I felt it myself. It was probably mostly in our minds, but there was a silent, eternal, waiting quality to the scene. The sun had dropped halfway into the ocean and had turned a deep orange, and everything on this side of it was in sharp silhouette. The horizon beyond was indescribably beautiful. Its coloring was orange around the sun and faded off in a great half circle into pink and lemon yellow, and finally violet and deep blue.

"You half expect a flock of ducks to rise off that marsh."

"Uh-huh," Pete said, "but right now ducks are nothing but an idea in evolution's file cabinet marked, 'Things to be done.'"

Suddenly goose pimples flared all over me, but not from the cold. They were from an idea not filed away but right up there in my mind.

"We're sitting here," I said, "but we're not even born yet. That makes everything real crazy."

"No, it doesn't," Pete replied quietly. "It just proves that the knowledge we base all our so-called truths on is faulty. It's what we see or think we see that's crazy. Not truth. Not reality."

"Uh-huh. Do you suppose we'll ever *really* know?"

"I doubt it. Man keeps discovering truths — truth here — truth there. But always *a* truth. Never *the* truth. Do you get what I mean?"

"I think so," I said.

"In areas like this you've got to fall back on philosophy. Exact science isn't big enough."

"You know something? That's all very beautiful out

there, but I'd give a year's allowance to see a few gaudy neons flare up."

"You and me both," Pete said in a suddenly small voice. "What *are* we doing here?"

It was getting *too* philosophical — too somber.

"We're here to find your dad, and we've got to get some sleep so we can start looking in the morning."

"That's for me. You sleep. I'll take the first watch and wake you up in four hours."

"Make it two."

The ledge we'd chosen was about four feet deep under an overhanging boulder. It was blocked at both ends and made a nice comfortable platform, with only the open side at the top of a steep fifteen-foot climb to defend.

We would be above the head of the tyranno if he came back, but we wouldn't know if he could get at us unless he tried. The winged lizards would have had a hard time getting a foothold to attack. With our rifles and automatics and hunting knives we weren't exactly helpless.

Pete took the first watch and woke me up in two hours. I took the second and let him sleep three hours.

Then something happened to our discipline, and the routine went to pieces. We didn't know this until we opened our eyes at the same moment to find daylight on all sides.

And a face peered over the edge of our shelter. We both had a moment of the purest fright possible — at least I did. A voice said, "Wake up, sleepyheads. A fine pair you are."

And we blinked, and were looking at Doc Tom and the big grin on his face.

Serpents with Wings

THAT REUNION was something to remember for a long time. First, there was a quick and joyful loosening up of everything. Pete jumped up from where he'd been sleeping and reached Doc Tom, who had one knee on the ledge. Pete grabbed him and pulled him up, and they went into a clinch.

Pete didn't exactly break down, but he was as close as you can come to hysterical joy without falling into it like a kid into a swimming pool.

Then Doc Tom held Pete off and smiled and said, "Glad to see you, son."

Pete gulped. "The same here, Dad."

"How are you, Bob?" Doc Tom shoved out his hand and I shook it, and nothing had ever felt so good to me before.

"Very smart of you to fire your guns as a signal," he said.

Pete and I glanced at each other guiltily.

Pete said, "As a matter of fact, Dad, we didn't."

"He means we didn't fire the gun as a signal. We were driving off a snake."

"One thirty feet long — a foot thick. It chased us out of the forest. Bob saved my life."

"Not exactly. We just found out that the serpent wasn't willing to scratch his belly on rocks to get to us."

Doc Tom was pretty perceptive. He appeared to grasp what had happened. "Smart thinking," he said. "But a sea serpent. I haven't seen any. I wonder what it was."

"We had a visitor, too," Pete said. "The big boy himself. Tyrannosaurus Rex."

Doc Tom's eyes widened. "I envy you!"

"Frankly, sir," I said, "you can have him."

"The meat eater. I've seen a few of the harmless ones — the vegetarians. They're all here, I'm beginning to think. And I'm starting to take a dim view of the period divisions taught in our later world. So far, aside from the fact that this *is* the world of dinosaurs, I've disproved more than I've verified. Now it's sea serpents — h'mmm."

Pete was grinning like a kid on Christmas. "Dad, it's great to find you."

Doc Tom was staring thoughtfully into space. "Allosaurus is here, and Tyrannosaurus Rex, along with the peaceful bronts, which is as it should be — but sea serpents — they're a *real* surprise!"

"Dad, we were worried sick about you."

Doc Tom jerked his mind back quickly. His expression said, "Worried? For heaven's sake, why?"

But it was the paleontologist talking, and that part of

him faded back when the father intruded. "I know, Pete. At first, I was alarmed when I found you and Bob here. I thought someone might come, but I didn't expect you two. But then I was overjoyed." He smiled. "Finding you alive and uninjured certainly helped." He slapped Pete on the back briskly. "And now how about a hot breakfast?"

"Did you say *hot?*" I blurted.

"Exactly. Some eggs I found. They have quite a gamy flavor, but I think they're delicious. I'm sure you will too."

"Let's get down off this shelf. Where are you camped, Dad?"

"Over in the rough country; I find it more practical and safer."

"We were going to head in that direction this morning," I said as I climbed down after them.

"I spent the night on some rocks back behind you there and started hunting for you at sunup. Last night I followed the shots immediately, but it was dark when I got here. I had to estimate your location, of course, but I was lucky."

"And smart too," I added silently. The whole aspect of this trip back into time had changed for me now. Pete and I weren't groping any more. We were with a professional who was more likely to know his way around in this time period than anyone else I could think of.

"This way," Doc Tom said, pointing toward the rough country. It looked as though we would be moving away from the sea and the forest, but Doc Tom said, "That water over there seems to be a vast bay. It curves, and we're moving roughly around the curve. We never get far from it." He took a few more steps and then glanced back and slowed down to wait for us. "Nor far from it or its dangers," he said with a slight change in his voice.

"You feel that the sea and swamps and forests are more dangerous than the dry rocky country, sir?"

"Definitely. Water always supports more life forms — a greater variety of them. You had an experience that tends to prove that."

"You're not kidding!" Pete muttered.

"Take it easy and watch the sharp rocks," Doc Tom said. "We've got a two-hour hike ahead of us."

On the way we discussed our technical difficulties.

The tunnel.

"My arrival was safe enough," Doc Tom said, "and quite uneventful. I arrived on a dry, sandy plateau over there on our left —"

"Then we can start plotting the tunnel's arrival pattern," Pete said. He hadn't stated it in so many words, but I got the idea Pete wanted to get to the freezers and the TV's and the comfort of neons flashing in the night.

"I've been plotting it," Doc Tom said. "I've seen it arrive several times, but could never reach it in time."

I asked, "Do you think Dad has figured out what our difficulty is at this end?"

"He probably has. He's had time to put all the data into the computer. I know he'll be annoyed by the miscalculation in the arrival problem, but —"

"Pete coined a word for it. He called it 'slippage.'"

"A very good term," Doc Tom said. "Of course it could have been calculated at the other end, but the job would have been enormous. And it really wouldn't have helped us much here. Being on the scene, we can trace it more quickly through observation."

I told him about the twenty-four-hour minimum span bit and the trouble they'd had at the other end after he left.

"What sort of pattern has the tunnel made, Dad?" Pete asked.

"It's a westward arc, but something else has turned up to complicate it a little. Even if we know exactly where it's going to arrive, we may still have to wait until it comes back to land."

"What do you mean, sir?"

"The gradient factor works perfectly. The tunnel will not arrive in water, but it arrives *on* water. It made three of its arrivals in an arc about four hundred yards out. I stood on the shore and watched."

"But you weren't able to trace it to where we arrived?"

Doc Tom frowned. "There was a variable. It may have been caused by the land-water factor. Anyhow, I lost it."

"Maybe it was because of the forest," Pete said. "Some area it rejected. It wouldn't arrive in the woods."

"That could have been it," Doc Tom said. "But now that we have your arrival spot to work from, I think we'll be more successful." He glanced at his watch. "We have almost six hours to wait for the next arrival. We'll cut across from my camp to where the general area has to be. I doubt it we'll get close enough to enter it on the next try, however — which," he added with satisfaction in his voice, "is perfectly all right."

"All right?" Pete echoed.

"Yes. I want to stay a little longer. I'm gathering invaluable data. It would be a crime to go rushing back."

"But Dad will worry," I said.

"We'll see how things work out. I think probably I'll send you boys back with a report."

That changed the whole aspect of the thing. I didn't want to go back! I wanted to stay around. And I could see by Pete's face that while he wasn't so hot for the country, he didn't want to leave his father.

"Couldn't you send a note?" Pete asked. "A report?"

Doc Tom laughed. "I was wondering how soon you'd think of that. I — "

Doc Tom froze. Then he reached out and gripped Pete's arm. "Those rocks there! Quick! Head for them!"

His order was so sharp that we were moving before we had the least idea what it was all about. The rock pile was about fifty yards away, but before we reached them we'd both seen the danger Doc Tom had spotted.

A big flying lizard was coming silently in from our left rear. It was a hideous thing, its evil intent written in its whole incredibly bony image. There was no doubt in our minds that it was after its breakfast.

Doc Tom rapped out orders like a drill sergeant. Cool as ice, he waved us down and said, "We'll crouch here — against this rock wall. It will have to angle in and it will be at a disadvantage. Get out your .45's."

We crouched there in a line, gripping the butts of our automatics and waiting for the next order. I don't know whether the flying lizard knew it had been spotted or not, but now it gave out with a thin squawk of rage. It wasn't quite like the one that had flown over Pete and me, but it was essentially the same.

Hideous.

"A Pteranodon, I think," Doc Tom said. "I want you boys to let it get about fifty yards from us before we start pasting it. You'll notice its left wing is exposed from this angle. I want you to point your fire at the joint where the wing is fastened to the body. Don't waste rounds firing at its head. The chances of a hit are too slim."

I'd always admired Doc Tom, but now my admiration went up a few notches. He wasn't in the least flustered, and seemed totally without nerves. He could have been explaining a problem to a class in a schoolroom.

I put my eye on the flying serpent and raised my gun and kept it trained on him. I was seeing the grotesque thing, but was still hardly believing him. He had a wing-spread of over twenty feet, and I got the weird feeling I was watching an old movie on TV — one about the pre-historic world — and in a minute the action would break for a commercial.

Have you tried the new wonder product: Zizzleswump?

"Now!" Doc Tom said. And we commenced firing.

I guess it was never going to stop being weird. The three automatics began bucking in our fists, and chunks of lead that wouldn't even be formed for eighty million years began slamming into a flying reptile that would be dead and gone long before the guns that fired the slugs were due to be invented.

It was a little like sitting in on creation itself.

We didn't do badly. Or maybe Doc Tom didn't do badly. Anyhow, enough of the slugs went home to smash the wing joint of the huge bird. It was like the wing falling off a small plane. The bird screamed in added rage and pain, and its trajectory veered sharply downward and to the left.

The other wing flailed violently, but it was not enough, and the bird hit the ground out in front of us, a hundred feet off its target.

Pete jumped up with a whoop of triumph and started forward. Doc Tom barked sharply.

"Pete! Stay where you are!"

The command brought Pete up sharply.

"It's down," Doc Tom said, "but it's got legs. It can still kill us."

And that was what the Pteranodon planned to do. An elemental life form, it probably had a pretty high pain threshold. At least, there hadn't been enough pain to stop it. Its only problem was the dragging wing as it came to its feet and started off. It was as clumsy as could be imagined. But it did move. And it still wanted its dinner.

"The left leg now," Doc Tom snapped. "Break it."

Again, I think it was his shot that did the job. The leg snapped. And again it was like a falling plane still on its own momentum as the flying serpent began in a circle around itself — hopping on its good leg and screaming at us.

We got up and walked forward with Doc Tom. There was both interest and compassion in Doc Tom's face. "All right, old fellow," he said. "You've had enough hard luck for one day. We'll put you out of your misery."

A few moments later the last shots were echoing and the

bird lay dead. Both Pete and I rushed forward to examine it, but Doc Tom's sharp voice stopped us.

"No time. Those shots might bring a whole flock. We've got to get out of here."

We pushed on, going fast and watching the sky. Way back on our right flank and very high, three specks appeared. Then two more on the left. We hurried on.

"How well can they see, do you suppose?" Pete asked.

"Well enough to spot us, I'm sure," Doc Tom said. "Swing over to the west a little. It's out of our way a bit, but that pile of rocks we'll pass might come in handy."

When they started down there were at least a dozen of them, and with Doc Tom's camp still half a mile away, it looked as though we wouldn't make it. I began wondering how well we could ward off a whole battalion of those ghastly sky fighters.

But we got a break. Possibly responding to an operational instinct that would later be a characteristic of high-flying vultures and other scavengers, the birds reached the scene and began circling. We could hear their screams way up in the blue, and I noticed they seemed to center on the spot behind us.

Then I understood. Their objective, or at least one of their objectives, was the bird we'd killed.

Doc Tom looked up at them and said, "We'll chance it. Run. Follow me. I'll show you the way."

We kited out across open country, and I could almost feel those long vicious beaks driving into my back.

"There," Doc Tom said, and we saw the rock pile where his camp was located. "Faster," he said.

I glanced back and up and saw that the flock had split.

Half of them were settling for what was easy — the dead bird — but the others were gamblers and were coming for us. And they were coming fast.

Almost too fast.

We dashed up to the rock pile and Doc Tom yelled, "In there. It's a cave. Scramble!"

Pete dived in first, into an entrance that was only big enough for one. I followed him, and the concert of raucous abuse from above was practically on top of us as Doc Tom threw himself in after us.

There were great clatterings of wings and screams of frustration outside, but we were safe. The entrance was too small for birds even half their size.

We lay there gasping for breath, unable to speak. Then I asked, "How long do you think they'll stay?"

"I don't know," Doc Tom said, "but I have a feeling we won't go hunting for the tunnel on this trip. We'll have to postpone that little chore.

The racket quieted down. We waited fifteen minutes before Doc Tom checked. He moved slowly into the narrow cave entrance.

Then he came desperately crawfishing back as pandemonium broke loose outside.

His fact was grim. "Two of them," he said. "Sitting out there waiting."

I dredged up some semblance of a grin. "Now I know how a prairie dog feels when a coyote watches at his hole."

"Oh well," Doc Tom said cheerfully. "They can't stay there forever. Let's fry some eggs."

They stayed all night. At least I woke up around four o'clock and heard them arguing in flying serpent language.

Doc Tom awoke at the same time, and yawned and said, "I'm surprised that they have developed such retentive faculties at this early stage of development."

"Suppose they're still there tomorrow, or when it gets light?"

"We'll face the problem when it faces us," he said. "Go back to sleep."

I silently thanked Doc Tom for having the foresight to select a safe hide-out, and went back to sleep.

And what he said was a good lesson in how to save yourself worry. The Pteranodons were gone the next morning.

But if I thought that ended our troubles, I was in for a surprise.

They were just starting.

Disaster

THE NEXT DAY we killed our first and only dinosaur. It happened this way. When Pete and I woke up, stiff and sore from that cramped cave, we found Doc Tom gone.

This panicked us a little, because our first thought was that one of those overgrown sparrows had pulled him out and eaten him for breakfast.

But when I stuck my nose out, I saw him sitting with his back propped against a rock doing some calculations.

"Good morning," he said. "Our friends got tired of waiting. How did you sleep?"

"All right, I guess."

"Well, you and Pete better have a quick cold breakfast

71

and then pack. I've been working on the tunnel pattern, and I think I have its next appearance spotted."

"You think we can get close enough to enter it?"

"I don't know, but we've got to be ready."

He hadn't said anything about packing for himself, and I thought he was still probably of a mind to send us back.

I was right. He said, "I'll stay around for another week, but this is too dangerous for you two."

I knew there was no use arguing. It would have been a waste of energy. We did what we were told, and an hour later we started off across the rocky desert.

We were careful always to keep a rock pile within quick running distance, but we didn't see any of the flying reptiles. Evidently they'd found better hunting elsewhere.

After about an hour we were back at the spot where Pete and I had first arrived.

"O.K.," Doc Tom said. "If I've got things figured right, we go in this direction," and he led us toward the rising sun.

After a while we were on the shore of whatever ocean it was that stretched to the horizon in that direction. There was no forest there, only open grassy plain with groves of trees spotting the plain, much as the rock piles had spotted the surface of the desert.

Doc Tom was frowning as he made some final calculations on a pad. "It never occurred to me," he said, "that surveying equipment would come in handy on this jaunt. But it's what we need to calculate exactly."

"We're awfully close to the water," Pete said.

"That's true. We may have to stand here and watch the ring appear out there offshore."

It didn't work out that way though. When the ring appeared, it was near enough to us to prove the real brilliance of Doc Tom's calculations.

But that was later. We had almost an hour to wait, and we spent the time examining our surroundings. The beach was about what we would have found at home. There wouldn't be much change in the next eighty million years so far as that was concerned. There were even very old-looking shells in the shallow water.

Evidently nature had finished experimenting with oceans and had about what she wanted.

The trouble came suddenly. Pete and I were at the water's edge, looking for some interesting specimens to take back with us.

Suddenly we were running back from the shore as fast as our feet would take us. A serpent has risen out of the water some hundred yards offshore.

"Snake!" Pete yelled. "The big snake again!"

I ran right along with him, but I'd seen enough of the monster to know he was wrong. It wasn't the same kind that had chased us out of the forest.

This one was long and straight and gray, where the other one had been twisted and coiled and garishly multicolored. The one that reared up there was frightening, but it didn't look as vicious as the other one.

Doc Tom had walked away from the shore to examine some soil, and he waited for us there.

"Run," Pete yelled. "Snake after us."

But Doc Tom didn't seem at all frightened. He stood there looking behind us and sucked thoughtfully on his pipe.

"No, Pete," he said. "It's a Brontosaurus. The only way it could hurt you would be to step on you. It's not a meat eater."

We looked back and saw the rest of it. It was coming up out of the sea, and what we'd thought was a snake turned out to be the bront's neck. Now its whole body was in view.

We gaped at the thing. "Wow!" Pete muttered. "It's a walking mountain! It must be fifty feet long."

"More than that, I'd say, from the head to the tip of the tail," Doc Tom estimated. "And there can be hardly any brain at all in that head. He has another one at the other end of his body that tells his tail what to do."

Doc Tom was watching it as calmly as though he were studying a cow in a pasture back home. "About all its brain can do for it is to warn of danger and keep its jaws moving while it eats."

The bront had stopped and was looking stupidly around. A body like a blimp on four thick legs.

"It lives on underwater grass and vegetation," Doc Tom said. "But the wonder is how it can get enough food down that narrow throat to support its body."

"Hadn't we better, kind of — leave?" I asked.

"I don't think we're in any danger." Doc Tom pointed with his pipe. "The bront's enemies are the meat eaters, like the Allosaurus. If they catch him away from the water, he's a dead duck."

The bront began lumbering ashore, and Pete and I moved back. But Doc Tom didn't seem to see the thing as a beast. It was more of a puzzle to him. He stared at it and said, "Nature made all its creatures vulnerable to some

74

other creature and then gave them defenses. The plant-eating dinosaurs went in two directions. Some of them grew shell-like armor, and others stayed soft and depended on the water for protection. They lasted for millions of years right along with the meat eaters, so their defenses must have worked fairly well."

Pete and I were more concerned with how well *our* defenses would work and how long *we* would be around. The bront was definitely coming ashore now, lumbering up on the beach and onto the grass. Its long neck was writhing around and swaying in snakelike fashion as it watched for danger. But evidently we were too small to be put in that class.

Doc Tom was moving slowly back with us. He said, "Don't be afraid. Just stay out of his way. He won't attack."

Then the big accident happened. The bront stood making up its mind what to do when there was the sound of a power hum and the tunnel appeared.

It arrived not ten feet from the bront, and the beast heard the noise and may have seen the ring, but more likely it had not.

Anyhow, it sensed something, and in trying to avoid it and get away from it the bront lumbered straight into the ring.

Its legs banged against the rainbow circle, and it wasn't a rainbow any more. Short-circuited, the high-voltage electricity flamed into eye-searing chaos.

Instantly fried by the electricity, the flesh of the bront was seared away. The animal gave out an oddly childish whimper of terror and the fried leg collapsed, bringing its huge body down onto the power.

It was like a giant roast. Barbecued dinosaur! The odor of the cooked meat filled the air along with the high-pitched bellow of the beast. It toppled over, the power reaching and searing both its little brains. The earth shook as it tumbled to the ground, some of its bulk thrust into the ring.

That was what we saw. But there were two ends to the tunnel, and although we didn't know it at the time, the accident was causing a real sensation at the other end. At that moment, their time, big chunks of bront meat, fried and sizzling, were being dumped out of the ring onto the floor of the platform.

We had our own troubles, however — our own tragedy. The ring's time period ended, and it vanished and there we were, stranded eighty million years from home. A long, long walk.

Pete and I stared, stunned into silence. But Doc Tom analyzed the situation quickly. "We've got to get out of here."

"What's the hurry now?" I asked. "He's dead."

"Yes, but the odor will bring every meat eater from miles around. We've got to head for the desert and keep our eyes open."

But it was too late, even though we were ready to start immediately. How the word got around so fast, I'll never know. We hadn't taken a dozen steps before those bony, winged lizards appeared in the sky. Then, seemingly from nowhere, a weird, lizard-looking thing came over the slight rise, blocking what would have been the path of our retreat. It was twenty feet long and ran on all fours. And I do mean *ran*. This wasn't one of the slow ones. It had a big lizard body with an armor plate of some kind covering its neck. It had two long, vicious horns protruding from the plate and a shorter one from the end of its snout. The overall image looked like sudden death.

And it was coming to the party.

"Triceratops, I think," Doc Tom said. "No meat eater, but still a killer. Come on! The water is our only chance."

We didn't stop to debate it. We ran toward the ocean, and Doc said, "We might be able to kill it with rifles, but there will be more. We wouldn't have a chance."

We started wading into the water as the lizard thing approached the dead bront. By this time a dozen birds were circling overhead.

We walked carefully and found the bottom solid under our feet, which was a blessing. That allowed us to stand rather than tread water, as we would have had to do if we'd found ooze.

We went out until the depth was up to our necks and then turned to look. It was incredible how fast the members of the feast were gathering.

Three more had arrived. But they were small. Ten-foot-long lizard-type specimens that may or may not have been classifiable.

Triceratops was temporary boss and was evidently only there out of curiosity. He didn't eat what was on the menu. He nosed the body of the dead bront and made some grumbling remarks in the native tongue and seemed to be just plain mean, keeping the others away.

"What about the snake that chased us?" Pete said nervously. "It was a water creature."

"We're not exactly safe out here," Doc Tom answered, "but we have to take the risk. I think — at least I hope — that your sea serpent belongs in the marshes and stays there. We've got to play it by ear."

A fourth creature had arrived, and the Triceratops was no longer boss. This new one looked like a mad artist's version of a turtle. It was about six feet long and had a rough shell over it. Its head was turtle-shaped, but more vicious-looking than any turtle you ever saw. It didn't seem to recede back under the shell. The thing had long spikes sticking out clear around the bottom of its shell. These protected its short legs, and it had a tail with a big hammerhead on the end.

It nosed up to the bront and sniffed, paying no attention to anyone. But the Triceratops acted as though it has sent out the invitations and the turtle thing was a party crasher. It lunged and rammed a horn at the turtle. The horn hit hard bone and didn't even leave a scratch.

"An Ankylosaurus, I think," Doc Tom said. "If we're right in our ideas, he doesn't even have to worry about Rex himself."

"He's not carnivorous, is he?" Pete asked.

"No. He's not eating — just curious."

He certainly didn't have to worry about the trice. He rumbled a protest, and turned and swung the hammer-tail. It smacked the trice on its head armor and sounded like a truck smashing into a bridge stanchion. The trice bellowed and rolled on its side. Then it decided that fighting for food you couldn't eat anyhow wasn't very smart, got back on his feet, and in order to save face took out after one of the squatting Pteranodons. The bird squalled angrily and dashed down the runway and took off.

Then the earth shook.

I don't know whether Tyrannosaurus Rex had a flare for the dramatic or if it was only the way it looked to us. But when he reared up beyond that hill off the beach, you knew one thing:

You knew the king had arrived.

He stood there with his big jaws open and his little arms hanging in ridiculous uselessness. He was twenty feet tall, and there were drippings off his jaws we could see from where we were. Maybe fifty feet long in all, but erect and contemptuously fearless.

The fiercest meat-eating animal that ever walked the face of the earth.

He came forward, and the ground seemed to cringe under him. There were a dozen or so nightmare beasts present now, big nightmares and little nightmares, and Rex walked through them as though they didn't exist. And they stepped aside.

As he arrived, the lesser ones backed away from the feast, and Rex bent over and set his six-inch teeth into the bront's flesh. His four-foot jaws came together, and he wrenched out a great chunk of the meat as though he were tearing a cream puff. Except that what he got was fifteen or twenty pounds of meat. A medium-sized bite for a tyranno.

The small meat eaters sneaked around to the other side, and Rex ignored them.

"How long will we have to stay here?" Pete asked.

"Let's start moving," Doc Tom said. "We'll go slowly and try not to attract attention. Watch for holes on the bottom."

We had to walk. We were too heavily loaded to swim, and we didn't seem to make much progress. But we kept at it, and the marshes — where the big snakes lived — drew farther and farther away.

So did the bront feast.

When we got about five hundred yards down, Doc Tom said, "Let's take a chance and go ashore. Maybe we can cut around them and get back to camp."

We managed it, passing one more guest — a negligibly small, five-foot armadillolike creature on its way to the beach party.

But it wasn't a happy homecoming for us, if Doc Tom's cave could have been called home. Pete was in terribly low spirits. Before we found Doc Tom, he'd been resourceful and self-reliant. Now, he hadn't changed exactly, but he seemed to have turned all authority back to his father and depended on Doc Tom for everything, including encouragement.

"Dad," he asked, "are we here for good?"

Doc Tom gave the question grave consideration. "I don't think so, Pete. That would mean that Sam Miller is abandoning his whole project, which isn't likely."

"But the unit back there could have been destroyed by the bront."

"That's possible. We have no way of knowing."

"It might take him a long time to repair it."

"It's possible."

"Besides, there's the money. He needed some from you

to finish the machine in the first place. If it's destroyed, he may not be able to raise the money to fix it."

Doc Tom did not reply directly. He lighted his pipe before he spoke. Then he said, "Everything you say is true, Pete, but I think we should look at it in another way."

"What do you mean, Dad?"

"Take a broader view. You know the dinosaurs died out because they couldn't adjust to what was, for them, a harsher world. We have come into what is, for us, a far harsher world than the one we knew. But we have the evolution of eighty million years on our side. Our ammunition will not last too long, but we have our superior intelligence and knowledge and resourcefulness to fall back on. We should be able to make out — indefinitely."

Doc Tom's words hit in two directions. They were inspirational, and bolstered our courage and self-confidence. But also they reflected his own doubts about how soon, if ever, we would get back to our own world.

We stayed at the cave the rest of that day, and the night that followed was the longest I'd ever spent. It had been the greatest adventure of my life to go back into prehistoric times — more exciting than I could describe.

But to grow up and live and die there: that was something else.

Like Pete, I began to yearn for the flash of a neon sign.

A Message from Home

THE NEXT MORNING things looked better, even though nothing had changed. Things always look better after you've slept on them. At least that's how it is with me.

After a breakfast of bacon and the funny-tasting eggs Doc Tom had found, we had a conference; but it consisted mostly of our listening to what Doc Tom had to say.

"I've plotted the tunnel to a spot about two miles northwest of the beach," he said. "Of course that location's based on a twenty-four-hour interval. If they tried earlier, it will be harder to find it; but we'll have to try. Let's head out and be ready if things work right for us."

We made the trip without any mishap and found ourselves on the edge of the desert, with another part of the forest looming off to the west.

And Doc Tom was phenomenal! He hit it within a hundred yards. We heard the faint hum and looked around quickly, and there was the tunnel!

We dashed in that direction, and it was then that we got an inkling of what had happened. The ring was very dim — all soft pastel — and seemed more of an illusion than anything else.

Doc Tom made his decision instantly. "Stay away," he said. "We don't dare risk it."

We stood watching the ring and feeling about as helpless as a person can get. But just as it faded away, an envelope dropped to the ground.

As I saw the envelope lying there, a crazy thought struck me. If it had had a postmark to identify it properly, it would have been priceless to a collector. The first letter delivered eighty million years through time!

But that aspect didn't interest Doc Tom. He snatched the letter up and tore it open, and Pete and I crowded in. It was typewritten and was over Dad's signature:

Bob, Pete, Tom:
I hope this letter finds you, and I pray that fatal disaster has not befallen you. The chunks of meat that came through to us yesterday give me a pretty accurate idea of what happened at that end. The destruction here is quite serious. The impact of the beast blew out most of our wiring system and cracked the cement base under the unit. Repairs will take time. I cannot as yet give an accurate estimate.

By working straight through, we have managed to put the unit back into "limping" shape. Bringing all of you back through the fourteen cycles is out of the question. With the amount of power we are able to apply at present we can move two of you at a time, but only through one cycle. The job will have to be done, therefore, in short hops.

If I judge Doc Tom's wisdom correctly, and I think I do, he will not risk using the machine when he sees the weak signal we were able to produce. I am assuming, of course, that this letter reaches you.

The situation is this: We will direct the tunnel back to you exactly twenty-four hours from your receipt of this message, at which time you will have decided which of you is to stay and wait for the next delivery. Then two of you will enter the tunnel and wait for the third to arrive as soon as we can generate power for the next trip.

I have solved the locational variation problem, but won't go into it because I'm sure Tom, if he is there, has solved it also. If you two boys are alone, it will be difficult to explain to you, so I have to take the chance that you already have the thing figured out.

My spirits are uneasy when I realize the peril involved, when I think that all I have done and all I have written is based on the hope that I will reach you.

But I *know* that you are still alive and that this *will* reach you.

God bless and keep you, Bob. I know that whatever happens, you will face it bravely, a credit to yourself and to me. This, I know, will also be true of Pete. So, wherever you are, our prayers and love are with you.

God bless you,
Sam Miller

We didn't say anything for a while. I couldn't have gotten a word out, and I turned away to wipe my eyes because I didn't want them to see any childish tears.

Then Doc Tom said, "Great guy, Sam."

He put the letter briskly into his pocket and that was that.

"Well, we've got a day to kill. What would you boys like to do?"

Pete surprised me. He said, "Let's sneak back and see how the beach party's going."

Coming from a guy as careful and sensitive as he, this was a reckless statement.

Then I realized I was doing him an injustice, almost as though I were jealous of his good sense and intelligent caution.

"Great idea," I said. "I'm with you."

I wondered if Doc Tom would veto the idea on the grounds that asking for possible trouble wasn't smart. But he said, "We came to see the animals and that's where they are. Let's go."

And I'll always be glad we did, because we saw something I sure would not have wanted to miss.

On the way over we had a minor brush with a new kind of bird, one with feathers. He was a mean-looking little character that winged in circles over us asking what we were doing there.

"An Archaeopteryx," Doc Tom said. He pronounced it Ar-kee-op-ter-iks, with the accent on the *op*. The name made the crazy-looking thing sound pretty important, and I guess it was, because Doc Tom said it was the first feathered bird on record.

"It was with this creature," Doc Tom said, "that nature first invented the feather. The others we've seen aren't really true birds. They all died out. But the archy was tough enough to survive."

The stupid-looking bird kept circling and squawking, and with Doc Tom looking up at it and classifying it so objectively, the whole thing seemed funny. It didn't have the least idea how important it was or what a responsibility it had, fathering — or mothering — all the birds to come.

We didn't want to use our guns, but I held mine ready as the bird made a halfhearted dive. Doc Tom swung at it with his hat, and maybe it was afraid of getting one of those precious feathers damaged, because it circled away and headed for the forest.

We moved on. Everything was very still; we heard no sounds as we approached the beach. Suddenly a thundering roar split the air and jerked us up short.

We stopped some fifty yards from the rise that blocked our view of the beach, and Pete and I glanced at Doc Tom. He considered for a moment and then said, "We'll slip up and peek over. But be ready to take off."

We made the last fifty feet on all fours, pushed our heads up out of the grass, and there was the scene.

About a third of the bront carcass was still there, but all the beasts were gone except two, Tyrannosaurus Rex and a bigger version of another we'd seen before — the killer Triceratops.

"It looks as though Rex has chased them all away except the trice."

He'd evidently just ambled in to see what was going on.

But Rex, thundering rage out of his great throat, told the trice to clear out of there fast. The trice bellowed, "Sez you!"

And the battle was on.

Rex didn't seem to anticipate much trouble. He lumbered toward the trice until he was looming high over the four-legged beast, and then tilted his body downward, the vast and savage maw open to close on the trice's spine and crush it.

But the trice saw his target straight ahead — Rex's soft underbelly. He lunged, and his middle horn went deep.

Rex's bellows had been nothing at all to the one he gave out with now. I'll swear it rattled the shells on the beach.

He backed away, leaving the trice's deadly saber dripping blood. The trice, not adept at footwork, stayed where he was while Rex seemed to be pawing toward his wound with arms too short to reach it.

He showed a vague intelligence by circling around the trice and trying to go in from the side. But when he charged, the trice's tiny brain had given it the score and the vicious horns were there to bore in again, two of them this time.

Again the going was too rough for Rex. He backed away, blood sluicing out of him. He bellowed and pawed the air. He tried to bend over far enough to bite the spouting triple wound that was producing something he knew little about: pain.

The king always wins, so the king is seldom hurt.

But he wasn't winning this time. Nor did he have sense enough to quit the battle. He came in again, and this time the trice, sensing victory, came to meet him.

But the vast, horned brute was overeager and missed his charge. His snout horn only grazed Rex's leg, and the tyrant lizard wheeled and came down with his deadly array of teeth.

They closed over the trice's spine just in front of his hips, and you could hear the crunch of bone.

The trice squealed in rage and pain as its huge hindquarters were lifted from the ground. Rex tried to shake the trice the way a big dog would shake a small one.

He succeeded in doing this, but his grip was not deep enough to hold, and the trice dropped to the ground. It staggered and turned, and Rex made a mistake. He did not try to avoid the lunge, gambling on being able to again get his teeth into the trice's spine.

He got his jaws over the wide back, but as he did so all three horns plunged deep into his exposed belly, and instead of closing his jaws to cripple the trice he opened them to roar out his pain.

That was fatal.

The trice dug in and drove forward. Rex backpedaled and bellowed his rage to the skies, the ground shaking under the two monsters.

Then we saw one of the horns come clear through the dragon lizard's body just below his right leg. He teetered and fell.

But the trice was trapped by his own hold. The horns refused to slide out easily. The four-legged beast went over on its side and got within range of Rex's slashing teeth. They closed on his spine, and the two monsters rolled over and over on the sand.

The trice finally tore loose as Rex's strength gushed out through the red-spouting butchery the twisting horns inflicted upon him.

The trice came to his feet and staggered away. His hind feet still worked, but there wasn't much coordination in them. The joint bellowing still shook the beach as he turned and labored off.

But the winner is always the one who can walk away, and that's what the trice was doing. Rex was through. He lay there threshing on the ground as though infuriated by the fact that he couldn't get up.

The king had been beaten, the blood sluicing out like water from a fire hydrant.

"Let's go," Doc Tom said. "They'll gather for the celebration, and we don't want to be in the way."

We hurried back toward the camp, not saying much. Then Pete observed, "I guess what we saw proves something: that no matter how good you are, there's always somebody a little better."

Doc Tom didn't answer. His mind seemed far away. After a while he murmured, "I wonder if that was the one."

"The one *what*, Dad?" Pete asked.

"We may have witnessed a fight that is known of — that is recorded in our own time."

"What do you mean?"

"In one of our museums, there is a Triceratops reconstructed from fossils. It bears the scars of just such a fight as we saw. It could even be the same one. We know it was that kind of fight because only Tyrannosaurus Rex could have inflicted the bone-crushing punishment that is recorded."

I wasn't too interested. Doc Tom had said, "When we get back. . . ." In my mind I qualified that to, "*If* we get back. . . ." Watching the battle of the behemoths had chilled me, somehow. My spirits were slipping, and I thought of that corny old saying: "This is a great place to visit, but I wouldn't want to live here."

Suddenly I was so homesick I could taste it.

I wanted to see Dad.

And it would be hours before we would even find out if the tunnel was going to function.

I plodded along toward camp, dragging my spirits behind me.

Old Longhair

BUT AS USUAL, the morning was better. In the morning you awaken to hope and optimism. At least that was how it was with Pete and me.

The hours did drag a little, but the sun climbed the sky, and we spent the last hour in the area where Doc Tom said the tunnel would appear. As the time drew near, he gave us our instructions:

"This is as close as I can figure it — " he said — "this two-hundred-foot circle. If we're lucky and things go well at the other end, the tunnel will show here in three minutes. I want you to stand about a hundred feet apart — just there, Pete, for you. And, Bob, you stand over there.

You've got your equipment and you're all set. When you see the ring, start running — both of you. Dive into it. I'll follow later. Wait for me wherever you land."

Pete was tense and worried. "But, Dad, suppose the second hop is a few million years off?"

"Anything can happen, Pete, but that hasn't blocked us yet, so let's assume it won't. There's no more time for talk. Good luck, boys. Now go to your positions."

I think maybe Doc Tom planned it that way, tight, so there would be no time to get tangled up in emotionalism and long good-byes. These were luxuries we couldn't afford. We took our positions and waited, tensed as though a starter were holding a gun over our heads for a hundred-yard dash.

"Dad!" Pete called out. "Let's risk you coming along too — "

"There it is!" Doc Tom shouted. "Get going."

He'd been incredibly accurate. The ring appeared about halfway between us — a little closer to Pete — and we were moving, dashing toward each other as fast as we could travel under our load of equipment.

Pete got there a few seconds ahead of me and plunged in. The last thing I heard was Doc Tom's voice.

"Faster, Bob! Faster!"

Then . . .

. . . it was freezing cold.

The shock of it knocked the breath out of my lungs, and I staggered and bumped into Pete, who was bent over against the arctic blast that hit us. The wind was a steady, level, howling drive with sleet that cut into our faces like fine gravel.

92

Pete and I pawed at each other and Pete gasped, "They were wrong. We've jumped everything. We're in the Ice Age!"

In the Ice Age.

Merely stated in four words it doesn't sound like much. You could even find a pleasant side to it if you were far enough away. Lots of snow for skiing, log fires, and tall white mountains in the moonlight.

You could, maybe, but we didn't.

Where we stood, already chilled to the bone, the words had terror in them. *The Ice Age.* Millions of years of sub-zero winds and cutting sleet and glaciers grinding down from the north to cut new patterns in the face of the world.

The exact opposite of the long, long summer: the one hundred and thirty or so million years when the world lay basking in gentle temperatures and was a comparative paradise.

But that was all gone now — so far back that your mind could not actually grasp the great span of slow time. All the strange creatures were gone. The two huge beach fighters we'd seen yesterday had been dead so many million years that they were beyond memory, their bones possibly buried deep under many layers of rock.

But none of this was important at the moment. The question was whether or not our bones would join them in the rock layers yet to come.

"There's got to be shelter somewhere," I gasped out. "A place we can build a fire."

"What with?" Pete gasped back.

We turned to face away from the wind, and held hands to keep from being separated. "We might as well walk away from it as into it. We're just as likely to find shelter."

One thing was sure: standing there talking about it — or rather, screaming at the top of our lungs about it — would be fatal, so we began to move.

And we were lucky. After we'd struggled along, braced against the drive of the wind for three or four minutes, Pete stumbled and fell.

What he'd tripped on turned out to be a cropping of a big pile of something. We forced our eyes open and looked at it. Maybe it was salvation, but we still couldn't tell.

I helped Pete get to his feet, and we began circling it and found that the wind probably drove from the same direction eternally, because there was a hollow on the other side. We were sure we'd found a rock pile covered with snow; and that proved to be true, because when we got on the leeward side we were able to crawl into a sheltered cave out of the wind. It was still bitter cold, but in comparison to the outside it was like coming into a warm living room.

Exhausted from the battle with the sleet-laden blast, we dropped to the floor of the place, our lungs pumping frantically.

After a few minutes we were in shape to look around.

Pete spoke first as he pointed to the floor in front of us. "We really did jump," he said. "Those are human footprints. This cave has been used for shelter before."

We came to our hands and knees and crawled to the prints he indicated. "They're human, all right," I said. "But whoever made them was barefoot. That means partially naked people. How could they have stayed alive?"

"Fire?"

"Do you see any signs of it?"

He shook his head. "Nor anything to build one with."

We were both shaking, but we had our heavy jackets on and were warmly dressed. Otherwise we would already have been frozen stiff.

"I doubt if fire has been discovered yet," Pete said.

I guess I was a little dazed from the shock of the sudden change, because his words sounded silly to me. It was as though we were actors in some stupid play, and in a few minutes the curtain would go down and the director would tell us whether we'd read our lines well or not.

"It's crazy," I muttered.

"Crazy or not, here we are," Pete said, "and we've got to do something."

"What?"

"Let's take a look outside."

We could stand up in the cave, and it had a narrow mouth that afforded the shelter. We went to the entrance and peered out.

All we saw was a gray, howling nothing, but at least we did see it. We'd arrived in daytime, and a little sunlight sifted through the thick cloud roof overhead.

"We might find some buffalo chips," Pete said.

"Correction," I told him. "No buffalo."

"I mean that was what they used for fuel in the early West. Dried dung. Maybe there's some around."

"It would probably be frozen instantly. And if we thawed it out — even if we could — it wouldn't be dry."

"Bushes?"

"I don't see any out there."

"And we don't dare go any farther than we can see or we might not get back."

We returned to the deep end of the cave where it was warmest and slid down to the floor with our backs against the wall.

"I was just thinking," Pete said. "Those tracks. I don't think barefooted people could exist in this temperature. That could mean that we're in a nearer part of the Ice Age. There may be seasons. Maybe this is just winter."

"And we're way north."

"Uh-huh. But that still doesn't help us much. We can't sit here till spring."

"We don't have to. All we have to do is wait for your father. He'll be here tomorrow."

I knew what Pete's silent answer was: "We hope." But neither of us dared say it.

"Sure," Pete answered. "That's all we have to do."

"And our next jump may take us clear home."

"It could."

"Are you hungry?" I asked.

"No, but I'm thirsty."

He reached for his canteen. I did the same, and we both got about two good mouthfuls. The rest of the water inside was frozen hard.

"I guess I'm not as thirsty as I thought," he said.

"Neither am I."

"Bob, if we — " Pete's jaw dropped. "Hey! Look at that!"

I looked.

"We're being invaded!"

It was a long, snakelike animal, and my thought was

how could a reptile exist in this temperature? Then I saw that it wasn't quite a snake. It had no head.

Then it was withdrawn.

Pete and I stared at each other. "It looked like an elephant's trunk," I said.

The thing was gone now, and we clutched our rifles and moved toward the front of the cave. If we were going to have to defend ourselves, that was the place to do it.

We found nothing, and this scared us even more. For several minutes we stood staring out into the sleet storm — into the flat, gray nothingness.

Then, from around the edge of the entrance wall and into our range of vision, came a monstrous beast. Not as big as Rex or the trice or the creatures of the Dino Age. But comparatively just as frightening.

Its front legs were longer than its hind ones and its back sloped upward to the top of its head, about fifteen feet. It was covered with long, messy hair and had a trunk and two long, curling tusks.

"A mammoth," Pete murmured in awe.

"You're not kidding," I said. "It stuck its trunk in here."

"Then he took a swing around and came back."

He was standing motionless about fifty feet from the cave entrance. "What do you suppose he's looking for?"

"A telephone booth, maybe."

"Very funny."

My hands were numb, and I had to look down to see that my finger was still coiled around the trigger of my rifle.

"What'll we do?" Pete asked.

Not to be outdone in the joke department, I said, "We could go out and ask him where the nearest hotel is."

"You ask him. If he says more than five miles, find out when the next bus comes."

There didn't seem to be much of anything we could do. We watched as the mammoth again lumbered through the storm toward the cave.

I raised my rifle, but Pete pushed it down with the barrel of his own. "What's the point in firing at him? He can't get in here. The walls are solid rock."

"He doesn't look mad at anybody," I said.

We'd started backing away to get out of range of the trunk if he investigated again.

But he didn't. He came close, and we could see one tree trunk of a leg outside the cave entrance. Then we could hear a big grunt even over the blast of the storm, and everything went black. And as our feeble light vanished, the rock wall of the cave trembled and shook. When that stopped there was silence.

"What happened?" Pete whispered.

"It got dark."

"Somebody shoved a rock over the entrance."

I snapped on my flashlight and trained it in that direction. The rock was covered with hair.

"The mammoth lay down in front of the cave!" Pete said, his voice shocked with alarm.

Whatever came, I knew we mustn't panic. "It's the leeside. He wanted to get out of the wind."

"But he's got us trapped!" Pete raised his rifle.

"Hold it. What's the point of blasting him? It'll just

make him mad, and maybe he can rip this cave apart if that happens."

"But we're trapped!"

"So what? There's plenty of air. And we aren't going anyplace." I said, having swung over to the mammoth's side.

But Pete still wanted to shoot, and searched his mind for a reason.

"Besides," I said, "it's warmer this way. Old Longhair is doing us a favor. Let's wait and see what happens."

Pete lowered his gun, and we went back to the inner end of the cave. We again sat down against the wall.

"I guess maybe you're right," Pete said. "We'll wait awhile." He sounded drowsy.

There was nothing to do, so we talked about everything we could think of, but mostly about home and things we did. Even the boring things seemed exciting now, and we wondered what the gang was doing and talked about that.

Then our eyes got heavy, and there were long spaces in our conversation.

Pete yawned. "You were right. It's warmer."

I yawned too. "Real comfortable. Maybe we ought to get forty winks."

"Good idea. I'll take the first watch."

"We can both nap," I said. "We'll hear that beast when it gets up. We're really not going to sleep."

"No," Pete yawned, "only rest a little."

The cave *was* warmer, and I realized that we had underestimated our power to adjust. It wasn't so bad. It was real cozy. My last thought was, "Man — he can adapt anywhere. Even in the Ice Age."

A Change in the Weather

"**B**OB — WAKE UP! Bob — "
The voice came through dimly to me. I didn't want to wake up; I was warm and comfortable.

"Pete. Pete-boy! Snap out of it!"

That annoying voice, like the sound of my conscience nagging me over past sins. Nagging Pete too.

Someone slapped me. I was angry. I drove a hard right to the jaw of my tormentor. But my fist wouldn't double and my arm didn't move very far, and I knew the straight right connection was only in my mind. In a fraction of a second I had a terrible fight with whoever it was and flattened him.

"Come on! Both of you. Snap out of it."

A vague pain cleared my consciousness, and I was no longer dreaming. I opened my eyes. But the other way had been better, because there was only confusion.

A fire where there had been no fire.

"Up, boy — on your feet."

It hurt. Needles were going through my whole body.

"Up!"

I staggered to my feet, and it hurt worse.

"I want you to start walking. Walk to the front of the cave and then walk back. Walk to the front of the cave and then walk back. Walk as fast as you can. And keep walking."

I looked Doc Tom sleepily in the eye and began to walk. To the front of the cave. Back to the fire. When I got there, Doc Tom was pulling Pete erect.

"Walk, boy."

For a while there was the pain, and long before it was over I realized what had happened.

Pete and I had come close to freezing to death in the cave there in the Ice Age.

Doc Tom got both of us moving, and I was soon sharp enough to hear the concern and fear in his voice as it echoed back to me: *Get up before you die.*

That was how it was. Our close call.

As I walked and got better, I also got a little light-headed, and I giggled as I thought how we might have fouled up the scientists of our own time:

Today a momentous discovery was made. The perfectly preserved bodies of two young males were found by Professor Egghead in a prehistoric cave. An ancient mammoth, faithful to the end, was found guarding the cave. The finding of the two bodies has turned the whole scientific world on its ear . . .

I got back to the fire. "The mammoth. It let you in."

Doc Tom had just got Pete moving. "What mammoth?"

"It blocked the cave."

"It wasn't there when I came. Are you feeling better?"

"A lot better."

"Then do some push-ups here by the fire."

Later, we had some rations and some of the water Doc Tom thawed out in the canteens.

"We were lucky," he said gravely. "The good Lord took care of us, because obviously we weren't able to do it ourselves."

"But I didn't have the least idea I was freezing to death. I knew I was cold, but the cave got warmer after the mammoth came."

"That's how it works," Doc Tom said. "Freezing to death is a quite comfortable way to go. It was sheerest chance that I got here in time."

"How did you find the cave? The sleet storm out there blinded us. We stumbled on it."

"There was wind, but no sleet when I got here. And the plain outside is pretty level. Also, for some reason the distance between the arrivals was shorter. That saved your lives, because I came in not too far away. But now that worries me. I'm wondering if the cycle has been thrown off."

The fire felt wonderful. Doc Tom had found some bushes and dragged them along after him. But even with the fire we were all very cold.

"The important thing is to stay awake and keep moving about," he said. "We must watch each other — see to it there is no dozing."

"How long do we have to wait before we try for the next arrival?"

"There have been developments at the other end. Your father has managed to make some repairs. This caused a little confusion at my end. I was ready and waiting for the arrival well ahead of time, and the tunnel appeared. It was stronger than before, but still far from capacity."

Pete shuddered. "It might have thrown you years away from us."

"I think Sam must have taken that into consideration. He knew we had separated."

The thought of what Dad was going through hit me suddenly and hard. He was blind — working in the dark — functioning as though we were still alive, but not knowing. Working with no idea of whether he was reaching us or not.

"When the ring appeared," Doc Tom was saying, "a note dropped out of it. But when I saw the note, I only had a few seconds to get into the tunnel, and stopping for the note would have made me miss it. So I came on through. I don't know what the note said."

"Then we're not sure of anything any more."

"Were we ever?" Pete asked.

"Sam probably explained the repairs he had made. One thing we do know is that he'll keep trying, and we'll go out and wait for the tunnel on the new cycle. If he doesn't come, we'll try the old one. I'm sure one or the other will work."

"In the meantime," Pete said, forcing a smile, "we do push-ups."

"That's right," I grinned, "and when we get back we'll be in shape for football."

"Uh-huh. But I hope we don't have to make an end run around that mammoth to get to the tunnel."

Doc Tom's eyes lighted up at mention of the mammoth. "We have a little time," he said. "I think I'll just have a little stroll around and see if I can get a look at it."

"No, sir," Pete said with a sharpness that surprised me. "You aren't immortal, Dad. You can freeze to death too. And we're not letting you out of this cave."

Doc Tom was surprised too, and there was a pause. Pete broke it. "Well, you said we're supposed to take care of each other. Would you let Bob or me go wandering around out there?"

Doc Tom laughed. "No, I wouldn't. Time enough to go out there when we have to, I guess."

When that time came, Doc Tom gave us implicit instructions. We would join hands, and he would lead us to where he'd plotted the tunnel to appear.

"How can you find the spot from here?" I asked.

"I marked the spot of arrival before I started hunting you. Another thing: the signal is much brighter now, and so we'll gamble on the three of us going together. I don't think that's any riskier than one of us staying here alone."

That one would have been Doc Tom, of course. He would have insisted on it. So we would have insisted on the gamble and overruled him if he'd changed his mind between then and when the tunnel arrived.

The time came, and we went out into that blasting, frigid wind. There was no sleet, but the sky was still leaden and overcast; and while we struggled against the power of the blast, I decided that of all the stages of earth's evolution the Ice Age was the worst.

"O.K.," Doc Tom yelled with his head close to our ears. "This is it. We make it or break it. Keep your eyes peeled."

We didn't spread out. We stayed in a group, and my hands and feet and face had long since gone numb when the ring appeared less than fifty feet from us.

It was beautiful! Those rainbow colors were the most gorgeous sight I had ever seen.

Doc Tom saw it fading in first and jerked at us. "Come on! Move! Hit the track!" he yelled, and we were racing toward that lovely circular rainbow.

He pushed us through and followed us. And . . .

. . . the weather changed.

I think it was those radical and abrupt changes that were the main key to the unreality of time travel. To land with a numbed, frozen body and chattering teeth on a soft grassy bank with a crystal-clear pool reflecting a blazing sun at one end and a lacy waterfall at the other made a person certain that he was dreaming.

"It's greener," Doc Tom said. Interested in the realistic aspects rather than the dramatic ones, the beauty of the place was lost on him.

"It wouldn't have to be very green to — "

"I mean greener than the Cretaceous period. The colors are brighter."

That was true. Here, there was brilliance. The sky was a deep blue, indicating atmospheric change of some sort over the millions of years. I'd seen the forest creepers and parasitic plants of the Cretaceous period as bright. But that had only been by contrast. Beside the deep crimsons and the greens and purples around us they would have faded into pale pastels.

"Where do you think we are, Dad?" Pete asked as he beat his arms against his sides to warm up.

Doc Tom was already taking off his heavy jacket, and I followed suit to let that beautiful sun pour its heat down on me.

"We're in the Cenozoic era, no doubt about that — perhaps in the top edge of the Pleistocene."

I wasn't too well boned up on those terms, but I knew Cenozoic meant Recent Life. "Then we can't be more than a million years out."

"Probably much closer than that. I'd say about 20,000 years."

Doc Tom had seen the tracks in the Ice Age cave and hadn't been too excited about them, although he would have liked to have stayed around and met the people.

In every way we could anticipate, though, this was better. After the long summer, a hundred and thirty million years, and the long winter to remind the world everything couldn't always be easy, mother nature had relented and made it spring.

We stayed where we were, soaking up the heat we'd lost; and that night, under a gorgeous full moon, we realized the sky was all crazy. None of the stars we knew, nor any of the galaxies, were where they belonged.

"Don't worry about it," Doc Tom said. "Things will straighten out. You've got to remember that the sun circles our galaxy every two hundred million years."

"That's some trip," Pete yawned and rolled over to go to sleep.

"Sack out for a while," Doc Tom said. "I'll stand watch."

"O.K. Wake me up in a couple of hours. Then I'll pass the watch on to Pete."

Doc Tom didn't wake us up. The rain did. As I came to, I got the idea I was struggling to stay afloat in a swimming pool. Pete and I both sat up.

We found that Doc Tom had stripped down to his shorts and wasn't at all upset by the rain.

"It's a lot better than the sleet, isn't it?" he asked.

We had to admit that it was, but we would have still appreciated some shelter. But Doc Tom advised against sloshing around in the dark, even though we did have our flashlights.

"We don't know what we'll find, and it's better to face it in the daytime."

The rain fell for another twenty minutes and then stopped, as though someone up there has turned off a spigot. When the moon came out again, it was beautiful.

Doc Tom lighted his pipe and said, "Oh, by the way, Pete, happy birthday."

Pete's eyes widened. "It's my birthday! I'm eighteen years old!"

"That's right, Pete."

"But I haven't even been born yet!"

Doc Tom reached over and ruffled Pete's wet hair. "Maybe you haven't been born yet, son. But that's the way to bet it. Go back to sleep, both of you. I'll handle things until morning."

It wasn't quite fair to let him do it, and I resolved to wake up after a quick nap and take over. It didn't work

107

out that way. We went to sleep, and the next thing we heard was drums.

There was no twilight zone. Pete and I both came erect at about the same moment, our senses alert. The drumbeat was rhythmic and had a rumbling quality to it, and I got a feeling that it wasn't so much a signal as someone merely enjoying himself.

Doc Tom was unexcited. He'd dressed and had also caught several fish from the pool. He didn't seem to be worried about the drums. "O.K., sleepyheads," he laughed. "If the smell of this fish frying hadn't awakened you, I guess it would have been hopeless."

The fish made the best breakfast I'd ever eaten. There in that small corner of paradise that we'd found, the drums seemed to be an intrusion, and neither Pete nor I wanted to be the first to act concerned about them. I told myself they weren't sinister at all, only some guys out in the jungle having fun.

I don't know whether Doc Tom was playing a game with us or not, but he ignored the drums. But after a while, with breakfast almost finished, Pete couldn't hold out.

Picking a bone out of his last piece of fish, his voice was carefully casual as he said, "What do you think it is, Dad?"

I was glad he'd asked. Pride had made me hold out, but I was plenty worried.

"I don't know, Pete," Doc Tom said just as nonchalantly. "We can certainly bet they're of human origin."

"Do you think they're dangerous?"

"I presume we'll find out."

Doc Tom was great! I knew he wasn't being casual for superficial effect. It was to set us an adult example and block off any panic we might feel. I don't think we would have panicked, but he still saw us as juveniles and conducted himself accordingly.

He had finished eating and was studying the layout of the place.

"We're somewhat trapped here," he remarked thoughtfully.

"Then maybe we'd better find a safer spot."

"I was referring to the arrival of the tunnel. That gradient factor your father invented is a tricky thing. It's a little like landing a plane. There are forests all around us, but the tunnel found its way into this open area. That makes plotting the next arrival difficult. It will reject any spot, even on the pattern, if it's already occupied."

"That does make it a little difficult," I said very cautiously.

Doc Tom saw through me and gave me a faint smile. "There's another technical point of interest. That first jump back covered a far broader time band than our second. The cycle seems to be shortening. At least it appears that way. Another one like the first, and we'd be thrown into the future."

"Is that possible, Dad?"

"When you're working with something as complicated as time travel, you can't say anything is either possible or impossible. Sam's research proved it impossible to our satisfaction. By every rule we know, the tunnel dead-ends in the present — that is, the present we left behind us. But we can't be surprised at anything that happens. Our progression cycles may change radically."

Which made a nice coincidence, because a few minutes later I was very much surprised at something that happened. Doc Tom had taken out his notebook and was making some calculations on which way we would go to find the tunnel's next arrival, when there was a great crashing sound back in the jungle. We froze. Doc Tom quietly reached for the rifle that lay close. We did the same.

Then a huge beast broke out of the forest at the far end of our open pocket and clumped into view. It looked more like a bear than anything else I could compare it with. It had a bear's hide and vaguely, a bear's head, but it had a tail that was a solid extension of its body, like the tails the dinosaurs used as third points of balance. Except that this beast did not use its tail for that at all.

The beast turned itself, like a tower with legs, revolving itself slowly. It was twenty feet tall.

"I thought all the big ones were gone," I whispered.

"Be quiet," Doc Tom whispered back. As the beast stared at us, he whispered again.

"Don't move. Don't move a muscle."

The Beasts of Paradise

THE GREAT BEAST looked at us for a while, and then reached up and pulled down a tree limb with a funny three-clawed hand and began eating the leaves.

We would have breathed a sign of relief if any of us had been breathing at the moment. At least, the animal hadn't charged us.

Under cover of the noise from its chomping jaws, Doc Tom said, "I think it's a Megatherium."

"A what?" Pete muttered.

"A Meg-uh-THEER-ee-um," Doc Tom spelled out carefully. "Noncarnivorous. A plant eater."

"It looks like a bear," I whispered.

"Actually it's of the sloth family. An ancestor of the creatures that hang upside down in trees."

"Helpless and harmless, then."

"Comparatively harmless, but not quite helpless. It can be a tough customer when it's aroused."

"Then let's not arouse it."

Doc Tom was frowning. "The appearance of that animal gives us a clue to where we are — almost up to modern times. The Megatherium died out about 10,000 years ago."

The way he put it proved that you can put a man into the past, but he continues to think in terms of the present. Adjusting your mind is harder than adjusting your body.

The big sloth went on eating, and Doc Tom said. "Some Megatherium bones were found in Kentucky before the West was developed. And Thomas Jefferson hoped that eventually some of the animals would be found alive. But of course they never were."

"How soon do you suppose it'll move on?" Pete said.

"I don't know," Doc Tom answered. "But let's not give it the idea it isn't welcome, or it might resent it."

The animal had stripped the limb it had pulled down, and now it bent over and nosed the grass. But it didn't like it. Then it stood like a dog with its hind feet kicking at the ground. Its weight and size and the long sharp claws on its feet dug up several chunks of sod. It nosed down and checked, but evidently didn't find the roots it was after. It let out a vast snort of disgust and, to our great satisfaction, turned and pushed off into the forest.

"Very inhospitable," Doc Tom smiled. "It didn't even bother to welcome us to its day and age."

112

"I'm glad it didn't," Pete said. "Maybe we ought to start hunting for the tunnel."

"That might be a good idea," Doc Tom said. "We'll head out that way. I don't know what we'll find, but it's the right direction."

I almost regretted leaving the place. It had everything — beauty — fishing — swimming. A great place for a vacation. But there was the excitement of what lay beyond, and when we plunged into the forest we were happy to find the going not too tough.

But we didn't find any open spaces. As we moved, the sound of the drums swung over to our right and stayed about as they were — not louder or fainter.

As we moved along, something seemed to be bothering Doc Tom. Finally he stopped. "It would be a shame not to check on what the human animal looks like in this world," he said.

I could tell from Pete's expression that he wasn't too curious. He wanted to get home to the neon lights and a cold Coke. But he didn't object.

Then two minutes later I went through one of the most terrifying experiences I'd had to date.

It was weird.

We were standing there, Doc Tom telling us about the big sloth, and I was looking at a spot in the undergrowth about twenty feet away. I saw nothing but the undergrowth. Then, without anything moving, my eyes translated the perfect camouflage of the foliage into something else — something my mind refused to accept for what seemed a long time.

It was a face. And as I was forced to believe it, the

hair on the back of my neck stiffened and goose pimples began rising.

The face of a cat. A big cat, the size of our tigers in the zoo. But this one was different. It had two ten-inch tusks curving down out of its upper jaw. And there was more pure hatred and viciousness in that face than I'd ever seen in those of modern jungle cats. The two motionless yellow eyes that blazed out at me were aimed straight at my throat.

I gulped, telling myself the thing didn't exist, even though I was staring at it and knew that it did.

I was afraid to move. Shifting one arm backward, I flapped a hand in Doc Tom's direction. At any instant I expected the beast to spring, but I was afraid to do anything that might hasten that moment. The rifle I gripped in my right fist seemed to be miles away. The movement of bringing it to my shoulder would have seemed strictly slow motion.

The next few seconds was an explosion from all directions. The creature sprang with a bigger snarl than any modern-day tiger ever gave out with. It came straight through the air. Those two saber teeth grew from ten inches to ten feet as the beast rocketed in.

There was the sharp crack of a rifle behind me, and the beast pivoted in the air in an agonized twist as the snarl keened up to a high-pitched scream of agony.

The cat dropped to the ground at my feet, and I had enough reflex working to backpedal and pull away. Three steps and I fell flat and rolled over in panic, trying to crawl away.

But the cat had forgotten me and was attacking itself at

114

the point on its haunch that the slug had entered. One of its saber teeth drove into its leg and another scream of pain and rage erupted as it continued to tear at itself.

Then Doc Tom's rifle cracked again. The cat went into a savage, revolving ball.

His third slug hit the brain and stopped it in the middle of a spin as it went lifeless.

My knees were too shaky to stand on, and I went down to the sod. Pete stayed frozen as he'd been from the first.

"That was close," Doc Tom said. And his voice wasn't casual. It was low and grim.

"What is the thing?" Pete mumbled.

"A Smilodon, I think."

"But it isn't smiling."

"The word is from the Greek. It means carving-knife tooth. A more common translation is saber-toothed cat. Those teeth make it a king of the jungle. Its bones were found in the La Brea tar pits in California."

"Well," I said shakily as I got to my feet, "that one was almost down my throat."

Once the danger was over, Doc Tom found the composure to smile. "If this one ever landed in the tar pits, there'd be quite a lot of confusion over the bullet hole through his skull."

"Suppose I was found there with his teeth sticking in *my* skull."

"We'll try to avoid that," Doc Tom said. "Do you feel like moving on?"

"Sure thing."

As we started, Doc Tom looked back regretfully. "I'd

like to take that head with me, but it's best that we don't overload ourselves."

We moved on. The drums were pounding monotonously. As we plowed along through the jungle, I could see that Doc Tom was beginning to worry.

"We're going too far," he finally said, "but I see no way to avoid it. We know the tunnel isn't going to arrive in this kind of growth."

"Then we'll have to keep on going," Pete said.

Doc Tom nodded.

And we moved on as naturally as though we'd merely crossed the path of a farmhouse or a milk cow in a pasture.

Perhaps, in some ways, we were getting used to our new environment.

But then it was suddenly proved that things weren't as simple as we'd been taking for granted. Suddenly, out of nowhere, we were surrounded. We'd heard nothing and seen nothing. But at one instant we'd been alone, and the next moment — or at least that was how it seemed — we were surrounded.

The people had come.

Savage Death

THE PEOPLE.

They didn't say anything, but only stood there looking at us. They were small and primitive and deep brown, and some of them were dressed. But some weren't. There were about two dozen of them.

They were armed with crude spears and clubs, showing that they'd learned how to pound and stab.

But it seemed that some of them didn't care for those methods, because there were a few who carried only tree branches thick with fresh leaves. Maybe their job, I thought, was to keep the mosquitoes off the ones who did not yet believe in clothing.

They were neither hostile nor friendly. They were nothing. They only stood and looked.

We stood and looked also, on the theory, I suppose, that

117

we were the guests and it was up to the hosts to make some gesture.

But they didn't see it that way, and I began to wonder if we were going to stand there all day. Finally Doc Tom said, "Let's move and see what happens. Do it casually and quietly. Don't make any move they might consider hostile."

I was willing to try, but I thought they might consider breathing as hostile when they found out we were doing it.

We took three experimental steps forward — that was one for each of us — and it was pleasant to find out that none of us was skewered on their spears or clubbed to death as a result.

They hadn't objected to Doc speaking, so he tried it again. "They don't seem to resent movement, so take out your automatics slowly. If there is a show of hostility, we'll have to defend ourselves as best we can."

We took out our .45's, but this didn't bother them. Personally, I was trying to figure whether shooting one or two of them, if they decided to jump us, would back them away. I had a feeling it probably wouldn't. They must have seen us as being like themselves, but they could still have reacted as they would have to a wild animal. I didn't know whether a barking gun would make them retreat or charge. One guess seemed as good as another.

We walked forward, and they walked with us. None of them had made a sound, and Doc Tom tried an experiment. He said, "We come as friends?" not expecting them to understand, but wondering how they would react to the words when formed into a question.

118

They didn't react at all.

"If we pay no attention, maybe they'll go away," Pete said.

"I doubt it," Doc Tom replied. "I think our danger lies in a sudden whim on their part. If we'd been animals, we'd have been attacked already. But they're confused. We're like no animals they ever saw."

"But if one of those spears is raised, do we fire?"

"We'll have to," Doc Tom said.

But whatever held them continued to hold. We walked. They walked along with us, some a little ahead, but most of them in a semicircle behind. When we stopped, they stopped.

And then we walked out of the forest into open country. Maybe they'd guided us, I don't know. Maybe that semi-circle behind had gradually arced us around in the direction they'd wanted us to go. Anyhow, when we came into the open, we saw their village ahead of us.

A little more primitive, perhaps, but it still looked like the straw-and-palm-roofed collection of savage dwelling places travel books on Africa and Australia are filled with. Shelter building and group living were obviously an ancient instinct.

"What now?" Pete asked.

"Let's wait and see," Doc Tom replied. We were all hoping that a fight wouldn't be necessary. Of course we had to defend ourselves, and the laws of survival prohibited our using spears and clubs as they did. We had guns, and we would use them. But we didn't want to.

After we moved out into the open and stopped, a pattern of action became apparent. The semicircle behind us swung around and grouped with the others, and they began moving toward the village. It was about fifty yards away, and as long as they didn't insist upon our going with them we stayed where we were.

Their eyes never left us as they approached the village. When they were almost there, another native, very old, came out of the largest hut. As he did so, other of the small, naked and seminaked figures appeared from the other huts.

"The ones that found us must be the warriors," Doc Tom said. "To their way of thinking, they herded us in. Now they're asking their chief what to do."

We could hear snatches of the conference, and the language, though primitive, was definitely a language. It was punctuated with grunts and gestures and pantomimes.

These last were easily translated. They were telling their chief and the other villagers how they'd herded us in at great peril to themselves. If I interpreted it correctly, they were lying like troopers. We'd put up fierce resistance, but they'd overcome us and driven us cowering into the village.

"What do you make of that?" Doc Tom asked.

"I've got a feeling they look on us as their prisoners."

At that moment there was a diversion. Another of those silly-looking Megatheriums — or maybe the same one we'd seen — ambled stupidly out of the forest some hundred yards away and began eating the leaves off a tree that struck its fancy.

This sent a stir through the assembled villagers. It

looked very much as though the beast was legitimate prey, a feast for the village. Some of the warriors started in that direction. But a clumsy-sounding word from the chief brought them back. He hadn't taken his eyes off us, and now he gave the word. One problem at a time seemed to be the judgment.

Knock the three two-legged ones over and then go after the one with the tail.

They started toward us, and there was no doubt about what they meant to do with their spears and clubs. We raised our rifles.

"Hold it," Doc Tom said.

As we braced ourselves and waited, Doc Tom aimed at the hapless sloth and fired. The animal dropped to the ground as clumsy in death as it had been in life.

I'm sure the sound of the rifle didn't bother the natives. And whether they connected it with the death of the animal, I couldn't tell. But they stopped and looked at the sloth in bewilderment.

I was watching the chief, and he seemed to be as bewildered as the rest.

I tried to interpret things as they happened, but I couldn't tell how accurate I was. Anyhow, the advancing warriors had stopped and were looking toward the dead animal with obvious attraction. They took tentative steps in that direction, their attention drawn away from us. They also watched the chief, as little children bent on mischief watch their parents.

They took several hesitant steps in this fashion, and when he made no motion to stop them, they suddenly broke and dashed, along with the other villagers, in that direction.

It was difficult not to get the idea that in this village it was every man for himself. They charged in on the animal and began tearing it to pieces. The ones who had spears used them. The ones with clubs beat holes in the animal's hide and then tore at the flesh with their hands.

The weak were pushed aside and the strong prevailed. "Nice table manners," Doc Tom commented.

I was still watching the chief. He was definitely a cut above the others, because he hadn't taken his eyes off us. "We can't stand here all day," I said. "Should we go up and try to talk to him while the army is busy?"

"We can always start shooting if we have to," Pete said.

Doc Tom nodded and we moved forward. We walked as though we had all the time in the world. The chief stayed where he was, doing nothing.

When we got close enough, I said, "How do you do? It's nice to meet you."

He didn't necessarily appear to agree; neither did he yell for his warriors. We quite plainly puzzled him. He looked at the rifle that Doc Tom had used to kill the animal, but made no move to touch it.

Then he seemed to make up his mind about something and turned toward one of the huts. He walked in that direction. We followed, and when he got there he turned to us and pointed to the door. He was either ordering us in or inviting us to enter, I couldn't tell which.

Doc Tom nodded and smiled. "Meet him halfway," he said, without taking his eyes off the chief and being careful to keep his voice soft and pleasant. "Sit down in front of it and try to look peaceful."

We smiled at the chief and sat down. He regarded us with what looked like thought. But he had to get busy with other matters — matters that had to do with his personal welfare.

He left us and went out to meet the first of the returning villagers. It was a warrior who had ripped two chunks of meat off the dead animal.

The chief appropriated one of them, and the warrior did not resist. He stood there and collected his bounty from everyone who came by, until his arms were full before he retired to his hut.

"That's interesting," Doc Tom said. "They accept his leadership on some basis other than brute strength. Obviously they respect age and experience."

That might have been true, but they certainly didn't respect women and children. When the children and the females got in the way, they got belted.

They didn't seem to mind, though. They took their lumps and stood on the outskirts, and when the warriors and the men took what they wanted from the animal, the weaker ones moved in to get their share.

"I think we ought to take our share of the spoils," Doc Tom said.

"The beast must be edible," Pete added. "I wonder what it tastes like?"

I was wondering too. With some of the excitement having died down, I realized I was really hungry. "Do you think it would be dangerous to try?"

"We can find out," Doc Tom said, and got to his feet. "Cover me, but don't shoot unless you have to."

He began walking toward the carcass, but there was no trouble. With his hunting knife, he was able to cut off some steaks that the duller tools had missed.

He brought them back and said, "O.K., time out for dinner."

The natives had dropped down in front of their huts and began devouring the meat, and their table manners were far from the best. They ate the meat raw, cramming it in as fast as they could chew it.

"Are we going to eat it like that?" Pete asked doubtfully.

"No, we'll build a fire. I'm sure it won't frighten them. They must know what fire is."

They paid no attention to the fire, but when we started to cook our meat it was something else again. They stared in wonder. Some of them even stopped eating to stare. They they grunted and gabbled at each other in what was a language of sorts. Also, they laughed. What we did was funny — spoiling our dinner.

Family life was a basic here, but it hadn't been refined to any great extent. The man sat in front of his hut and gorged himself, with his wife and kids looking on hungrily. He was grudging in what he doled out to them, giving them nothing at all until his own appetite was at least partially satisfied. Then he tore off small pieces of the meat and handed them out. Any kid that acted greedy or grabbed too quickly got belted.

All of a sudden chaos broke loose. There was a yell, and

the warriors jumped up from wherever they were and grabbed their weapons and started running toward the carcass. We looked and saw a new crowd around the dead beast.

"What does it mean?" Pete asked.

"Invaders, I imagine," Doc Tom said. "Those newcomers must be from another tribe. They're trying to drag the carcass away."

There were perhaps a dozen of them, and when they were attacked they stood their ground and fought. But they were overwhelmed quickly, and most of them fled.

Two of them had been wounded. One had his leg broken by a club and the other got two of the primitive spears in his stomach.

A concerted cry of savage triumph went up from the victorious locals, and they dragged the two unfortunates into the open space in front of the huts. They encircled them and began to beat them to death.

It was bloody and savage and shocking, with only one saving grace about it. The job didn't take long. With every warrior in the tribe fighting to get a lick in, the two prisoners lived only a short time.

And after they were dead, the ones who hadn't been able to score a hit because they'd been crowded out continued to beat the dead bodies.

When everyone's bravery had been satisfied, the last ones to slug the dead bodies picked them up and carried them into the forest. When they came back, the scene returned to normal.

The savage murders shook us. The steaks Doc Tom had broiled looked good, but Pete said, "I don't think I want any. I lost my appetite."

"Me too," I said. "Maybe I'll be ready by breakfast."

But I didn't think so. I didn't think I'd ever want to eat again.

"It was tragic, of course," Doc Tom said gravely, "but it teaches us something. It teaches us that we aren't dealing with amiable children here. These people are savages, and killing is a part of their way of life. We must remember that and be very careful."

Gina

Her name was somewhere between a peep and a chirp.
Gina, with a hard G, was as close as we could come.
We got acquainted the next morning when she visited us.
She was a pretty little thing and looked to be about eight
years old.

When we'd awakened, the tribe was eating again. They
had picked the animal almost clean and were finishing it
up. Gina was a member of one of the bigger families, and
that morning there hadn't been enough to go around and
all she'd gotten for breakfast had been a clout on the head
from Daddy.

I'd been looking in that direction and noticed how she

hadn't seemed to resent it. But she had sense, and instead of trying again she'd wandered away and come in our direction.

At first it was a little embarrassing. Doc Tom had commented on their nudity. "Modesty is something that hasn't developed yet," he'd said. "These people wear clothing only for protection from thorns and bushes in the forest. So when they don't need protection — no clothes."

Pete and I reddened a little when she came wandering over and squatted down to watch us eat, and I think Doc Tom got a mild kick out of our embarrassment. But the total innocence of the girl helped a lot, and we got used to her quickly.

Doc Tom smiled and handed her a slice of broiled steak. She looked at it curiously, but when she took it, it was warmer than she'd expected and she dropped it.

We went on eating, Doc Tom keeping a weather eye out to see if the natives resented the girl's visiting us. None of them was paying any attention.

The girl watched us like a bright, alert little animal, her eyes sparkling with interest. From her expression, I judged it was incredible to her that we could spoil meat by burning it and then eat the stuff.

After a while she got curious and picked up her piece of steak, and wiped the dirt off it and tasted it in a gingerly fashion. She immediately made a face and spat out the bit she'd nibbled off. But after she'd rolled the taste around in her mouth awhile, her expression changed. She got interested and took another bite. She didn't spit it out this time.

Doc Tom had been watching her silently. Now he pointed to Pete and spoke his name. The girl cocked her bright eyes.

"*Pie?*"

She knew it was a spoken name and got the *P*, all right, but couldn't get the rest.

"Bob," Doc Tom said.

"*Bie?*"

She laughed. But what she'd said figured. From listening to them we realized they spoke a kind of *ki-yi* language. They handled the hard consonants pretty well, but everything else seemed to turn into long *i*'s.

She pointed to herself, and we couldn't imitate the funny little burp that came after the *G* in her name, and we finally settled for Gina as being close.

Her interest in things reminded me of a bird flitting from limb to limb in a tree. It bounced all over, never staying in one place long.

As she became less wary, she got more curious. She reached over and pawed me on the chest, but before I realized she was interested in the buttons on my shirt, she was examining the tabs on Pete's bootlaces.

Everything was fun to Gina. She'd gotten a clout on the head for breakfast at home, but it was obviously a part of her way of life, because she'd forgotten it in the midst of new wonders she'd found.

And Gina was exceptional even in her own time, because the other children whom we had attracted hung on the outskirts at a respectable distance, watching us, wanting to come close and be friendly, but lacking the courage.

And we didn't encourage them. For the time being it seemed wise to remain completely negative.

After a while Gina grew tired of us and wandered away, and we were not unhappy to see her go.

"Good," Doc Tom said, "we've got some decisions to make. How do you two evaluate this situation?"

"It doesn't look as though we have anything to worry about from these people," Pete said.

I was inclined to agree. "I think our main problem is to find the tunnel."

"To do that we've got to explore," Doc Tom said.

"Then let's get going."

"We can try. Pack up and shoulder your equipment. There should be no reason for us to come back here."

But we weren't going anywhere. They allowed us to pack and get all ready to leave, scarcely paying us any attention. When we started to walk away, however, we were immediately surrounded by twenty-five or thirty clubs and a bristle of spears.

When we'd been brought to bay, the chief emerged from his hut and approached. He began to talk, but he might just as well have kept his mouth shut. It made no sense to any of us. He might have been angry, but again perhaps he was only trying to get his point over. And this point was pretty obvious. We weren't leaving — at least not without a fight.

Several times during his tirade the chief raised his arms in a gesture, as though he were pointing and firing a rifle.

I asked, "Is he daring us to fire on his warriors?"

"I think he wants us to give him our rifles," Pete suggested.

"If they wanted the guns, they'd try to take them," Doc Tom said. "And I don't think we're being challenged to a fight."

"What then?"

"I don't know. One thing is sure, though. To get free, we'll have to fight our way out."

"Might as well get it over with," Pete said.

"Let's wait awhile. I don't think they're afraid of our guns, and unless we were able to panic them we couldn't win. There are too many."

"But we can't stay prisoners here forever."

"No, but let's wait and see if we can't find another way. If we did manage to fight clear and get into the forest, they could still destroy us. That's their country out there, and they know how to fight in it."

"Do we go back to the hut?"

"For the time being, yes. We'd better wait. In the meantime I'll try to communicate with the chief and find out what he's driving at."

When we went back to the hut, they dispersed, picking up the day's activities where they left off. These activities consisted pretty much of nothing at all. They sat around and jabbered at each other. The women squatted here and there, and fussed about with their elementary housekeeping work.

Only the children did things familiar to us. They played, as children of all ages always have and always will.

When we returned to our hut, the chief seemed to think his job had been done, and he went back to his own hut. We sat down and re-evaluated things. Both Pete and I were impatient, but Doc Tom advised patience and also practiced it.

"I'll wait a few minutes," he said, "and then go over and present myself to the chief. We'll decide on our next step after we find out whether he'll talk to me or not."

But it didn't quite work out that way. My impatience making me restless, I moved around the corner of the hut into the shade and kicked the dirt awhile, and then sat down with my back against the wall to think things over. The sound of bird chirp was tinkling against the backdrop of my consciousness. I got interested in it because it didn't sound quite like a bird. I looked toward the bushes some fifty feet away and saw a face. But not a Smilodon this time.

Gina.

She was crouched under a bush making beckoning gestures. "I'm being paged," I said, speaking loud enough for Doc Tom and Pete to hear. "Gina is out there under that bush."

Doc Tom walked slowly to the corner of the hut and leaned against it. Pete swung around so that he could see from farther away.

"I wonder what she wants," he said.

"She wants me to come out there, that's pretty obvious."

Doc Tom was measuring the distance. "Let's take a chance," he said. "Walk in that direction. Nobody seems to be paying any attention to us. If they object, turn around and come back."

I didn't have to be told twice.

As I got to my feet, Pete said, "Maybe I'd better go along." He was just as bored with the stalemate as I was.

"No," Doc Tom said. "Bob better try it alone."

I got up and walked casually toward the bushes. And either they didn't notice me, which wasn't likely, or they didn't object to one of us leaving at a time.

Anyhow, I reached the bushes without incident and pushed through. When I was out of sight of the compound, Gina came to her feet.

"*Gie nie die?*" she said.

"Sure," I answered. "Me too. What's on your mind?"

She hesitated and pointed back toward our hut. "*Die tie pie?*"

Those weren't her exact words, but they were as close as I could come. Then I realized she was speaking Doc Tom's and Pete's names as close as she could. She wanted them to come too.

I shook my head. "No. One-man expedition. Me. You tell — show."

She got my idea and turned reluctantly away. She soon forgot about Doc Tom and Pete, and took my hand and began hauling me through the underbrush.

I don't know how far we went, but after a while we came out into open country. Gina kept on going another hundred yards, stopped, and began a pantomime. She talked too, but that meant nothing to me, and I stood there trying to figure out her gestures.

First she ran around in a circle, and then stopped and pointed to the center of it. Next, she swung her arms in a big circle, implying that whatever she was talking about was bigger than she was.

When I still didn't get it, she looked annoyed and ran

back to the woods and brought a handful of flowers. They were red, blue, orchid, yellow.

She stood in the middle of the circle she'd paced off and began swinging the flowers in a circle perpendicular to that one, while her bright eyes accused me of being a dope.

I finally got it and accused myself of being a dope for taking so long.

Gina had seen the rainbow ring! She'd watched the tunnel arrive and vanish!

Other ideas followed that. I was sure she had brought me out here to get an explanation of it. She knew none of her own kind could give it to her and sensed us as being more intelligent. At least, that explanation would do until a better one came along.

I wouldn't be able to explain it to her, of course, but this was still a tremendous break for us. Gina had shown me where the open country was, and I had a bearing from which Doc Tom could trace down a future arrival of the tunnel.

But her eyes were sparking with questions, and I at least owed her an attempt. I made a big circle with my hand and smiled and nodded and said, "Uh-huh. That's how it is," I pointed to myself. "*Bie — Die Tie, Pie*. We come."

I made a pantomime of stepping through an imaginary circle. "We go." I made a little jump and a walking gesture with two fingers along my arm. "Get it?"

I think she did, vaguely, because she was sharp as a whip. She laughed and jumped up and down.

I pointed toward the woods. "We go back now?"

I started and she followed, satisfied with what I'd told

her. And while she chattered like a primitive magpie, I smashed bushes and pulled up vines to mark the path so we could find it again.

We got back after I'd been gone about an hour, and I was briefed on developments back at the village.

"I didn't get anywhere with the chief," Doc Tom said. "What you've accomplished will be the key to our procedure. I still think we can get away without shedding blood. They don't seem to object to our going one at a time, so that's how we'll do it."

"I marked the path pretty clearly. There'll be no trouble following it."

"There's no use delaying. You go back the way you came and wait there. Pete will wander out next. We'll leave some of our equipment in front of the hut this time, and not make quite such a production of leaving."

There was only one rub. I couldn't get rid of Gina. She'd attached herself to us and that was that.

I accomplished one thing. Tired of roaming around with a naked child, I went into the hut and tore a sarong-sized piece off my blanket. I brought it out and made motions indicating that I wanted her to put it on.

She got the idea immediately, and because some of the females did wear costumes of various sorts, it wasn't a completely new idea to her.

She wrapped the piece around herself, and then she jumped up and down and laughed and clapped her hands and it fell off.

We put it back on and tied it with a tough length of dead vine that was as good as cord. I felt better.

"O.K.," Doc Tom said, "ease out quietly. Leave your

rifle. I'll try to bring it along later, but if I can't, you've got your side arm. Pete will come along in fifteen minutes. I'll follow soon. After we get clear, we'll just have to hide out until I can plot the tunnel's next arrival."

We were still burdened with Gina, and I didn't quite know what to do about her. She'd originally beckoned to me from the bushes, and it seemed logical the natives would resent our going off together in plain sight.

But it was a pleasure to deal with such an intelligent child. I looked at her and took a couple of casual steps toward the bushes and stopped. Her eyes flashed with understanding and she ran off, not in that direction, but at an angle.

I knew she'd be waiting for me when I got clear, and she was — like a kid playing an exciting new game.

We went back to the spot where she'd seen the ring and waited, and in a little while Pete showed up.

"It was simple," he said. "When we leave one by one, they don't notice. Dad'll be along shortly."

But he didn't come. Time passed. He still didn't come.

By the time we'd really started to worry, there was a diversion. I heard a familiar sound. The power hum.

And out in the clearing, a hundred feet from where Gina had paced off her circle, the rainbow ring came into view.

It glowed strong and beautiful, with all its old power.

Escape

WE FORGOT EVERYTHING and ran toward the tunnel. But when we got there, we remembered a few things and stopped. Pete's reaction came quickly.

"Jump through! Go ahead. Your dad must be plenty worried. I'll stick here and wait."

But I couldn't do it. "No, I'll wait too."

What Pete had said about Dad worrying hit me, though. I suddenly realized he was there in the laboratory, playing it blind. Why hadn't we thought to send him a message?

Desperately, I looked around for something to send, hoping maybe it would get there. The easiest thing to rip loose was my watch. I slid it off my wrist and tossed it through the ring, and at the same time something came back. Another letter.

The ring faded out.

As I picked up the letter, I noticed Gina standing back. Quite naturally, she was afraid of the ring, and she was set to run at the first flash of danger.

When it faded, she came close and stared in awe and bewilderment at the letter I'd picked up. She'd seen it materialize out of nowhere, and that in itself had been pretty frightening.

I started to tear the letter open before I noticed that it was addressed to Doc Tom, and I stopped tearing. It took a lot of will power to shove it into my pocket unopened.

Pete and I looked at each other and spoke at the same time. And we both said the same thing.

"We've got to go back."

Gina had stopped yakking in that weird tongue since the ring had appeared and vanished. I didn't know whether she was still awed or whether her mind was working on some idea of its own.

It didn't really matter. The important thing was what had happened to Doc Tom. He'd had almost an hour to get there. Maybe he'd gotten lost, but I didn't think so. The broken path through the jungle was well marked.

Had he been attacked by the natives when he tried to leave? I guess that idea hit Pete and me at the same time too. Neither of us said anything, but we both quickened our pace. We started running as fast as the jungle would let us.

When we got to the village and looked out through the bushes, we breathed a sigh of relief. There was nothing going on in the open area.

No bodies lying around.

But from where we were we couldn't see in front of our hut, and we were tense as we approached it. Then we saw something that was both good and bad. Doc Tom was there. Things were good because he wasn't dead. He hadn't been murdered.

But they were bad because he was a prisoner. Some kind of net woven from creepers and ivy stems had been dropped over his head and pulled tight. He sat there on the ground as helpless as a netted fish.

I ran forward, but Pete was ahead of me. With a cry of anger he jumped forward with his rifle ready. But Doc Tom's sharp voice brought him to a quick halt.

"Hold it! Don't get excited. That's the key to these people. Whatever you do, do it calmly."

"But, Dad. We can't let you stay in that net."

"Just take it easy, Pete," Doc Tom counseled. "Anything we can do can be done after we talk things over."

"What happened, sir?" I asked.

"I think I have them figured out. Their motivation. They saw me kill that animal with the rifle. That makes me important. It's why they let you two walk out. But when I tried it, they were all over me in no time. They put me in this bag, and the chief very carefully laid my rifle beside it. They weren't angry. I'm certain they're keeping me here to shoot more game for them."

"They didn't touch our rifles," Pete said.

"That bolsters my argument. They saw my gun used. That makes it important too. It's a part of me and my value to them. The other guns weren't used, so they ignored them."

"O.K.," Pete said. "What you say may be true, but it

doesn't change anything. We're not going to leave you in this net."

"Let's stop being so peaceful, sir, and get a little tough. Being peaceful is fine, but maybe we're overdoing it."

Doc Tom was frowning; he was struggling with a problem, and suddenly I saw what it was.

Us. Pete and me.

Doc Tom felt himself responsible for our safety, and for that reason wasn't even taking logical chances. I knew he wouldn't have been nearly so negative if he'd been alone. As it was, he was sitting tight and hoping that things would work out even if he had to sit in a fish net.

He wasn't going to do anything that would in any way risk our lives.

"As I see the situation," he said, "they'll have to free my net if they want any hunting done —"

I touched Pete on the shoulder. "Will you come here a minute?" I said.

I took Pete out of earshot and told him how I sized things up. He thought it over a few moments and nodded in agreement. "You're right. I should have realized that."

"All right, then our next step is obvious. We've got to kind of take over."

"But what do we do? Free Dad against his own orders and see what happens?"

"It's an idea, but I think I've got a better one. That way, if they jump us before we get him out of that net, he'll be lying there, helpless. Let's take our own rifles and start showing a little muscle."

"Kill some of them, you mean?"

140

"No. Not unless they ask for it. Let's show them what a couple of rifles can do."

"Dad will object," Pete said slowly.

"Sure, but as I said, we've got to take over — otherwise we let things drift. I think they've drifted far enough."

Pete made his decision, and I knew it was a tough one. Doc Tom would veto it, and that meant that Pete would have to go against him.

"All right," he said. "I'm with you. What's your suggestion?"

"Let's take our guns out there and play it by ear."

When we got back to the front of the hut, Doc Tom looked at us sharply. "What's up?" he asked.

Pete took charge. "The first thing is you, Dad. You're coming out of the fish net."

"Now just a minute —"

Pete took his knife out and began cutting the thing open, and when Doc Tom saw that he'd evidently made up his mind, he cut the objection off.

"Stand by, Bob," Pete said. "Watch for trouble. If they move in, try to keep them busy for a minute."

They came in fast, but I wasn't forced to shoot because they never did anything on the home grounds unless the chief was there. They threw the semicircle around us and waited. A minute was all it took to get Doc Tom clear of the net, and then there were three of us facing them with guns.

The chief arrived, and again I wondered what made him so powerful — something we never did find out. He walked into the open space in front of his army, and there was a very tight moment.

Then something happened that looked like the biggest coincidence on the books. There was sudden yelling from every direction, and the village was under attack by a hostile tribe. Savages swarmed in, brandishing spears and clubs.

The local natives forgot all about us. They flung themselves into the defense of their village with zest and enthusiasm. The three of us stood grouped in front of our hut, with Gina staying close.

One thing struck me. These people did not seem to know fear in any form. Gina's eyes were bright with excitement as she watched friend and foe go down in the fighting.

The clubs and spears were pretty effective at close range. One attacker screamed as he was skewered clear through, but soon the man who killed him was himself flattened by a club over the head, his skull crushed, because he couldn't pull his spear out in time.

At the peak of the fighting about two hundred men were mixing it up, with casualties on both sides.

We stood there gripping our rifles and Pete asked, "What about it? Is this our fight?"

With a crisis at hand, we'd turned the leadership back to Doc Tom automatically. He scowled at the primitive carnage and shook his head. "I don't think so." He lifted his rifle. "Except maybe to stop it if we can." And he fired two quick shots into the air.

This had an effect on the invaders, but it was to their disadvantage. Almost to a man, they stopped fighting. But our side had heard the rifle before, and they didn't stop.

One fanatic invader seemed to take the shots as a per-

sonal insult. He was the only one who came to investigate.
But he made up for several others with sheer mad ferocity.
His eyes blazing and his spear raised, he charged in.

I killed him. When he was some twenty feet away, heading straight for Doc Tom, his spear raised and about to be
plunged into Doc Tom, I raised my rifle and fired and hit
him square in the chest.

It was a snap shot, and I was lucky.

Later I tried to remember how I felt, but I couldn't.
That was when I started feeling guilty. I wasn't affected
emotionally. I was only relieved when he fell.

I guess that's what they mean by the "heat of battle."

I don't think the man I killed had anything to do with
it, but from that point on the invaders turned into losers.
Doc Tom was quick to notice this, and as my man fell he
was already pushing Pete toward the corner of the hut.

"This is our chance. Get going. We'll try to hide in the
forest until we can find the tunnel."

As we left, the invaders were in full flight in the other
direction, leaving our way clear. The last thing I saw in
the village wasn't very pretty. The wounded were being
stabbed and beaten to death as they tried to crawl after
their uncaring comrades. One thing was obvious. In prehistoric wars it was every man for himself. And it didn't
look as though anybody took any prisoners.

After we'd plunged into the forest, I glanced back and
saw Gina running along like a wood sprite, catching up
with us. I stopped and signaled her to go back, but it did
no good. The battle had been a lot of fun for her, and now
escaping with us was just as exciting.

She laughed and came on even faster.

The only way I could have stopped her would have been to tie her to a tree, so I gave up and hurried on after the others. They were out of sight.

As Gina and I hurried along the path, I couldn't figure out how they'd gotten so far ahead. When we broke into the open, I realized that they hadn't. They'd missed the path and were roaming around somewhere in that jungle.

This scared me plenty. A perfect plan gone haywire because of one little slip. And now, what to do about it? I'd never felt so helpless in my life.

Another frustration was even worse: not being able to communicate with Gina and tell her a simple little thing about two people getting lost.

I guess she assumed that everything always went perfectly for superior beings such as we appeared to her to be. When we reached open country, and Doc Tom and Pete weren't there, she seemed to think that was the way we'd planned it.

I tried to explain how wrong she was. I shrugged my shoulders and turned my palms up and said, "*Die Tie — Pie* — no here."

She laughed and shrugged *her* shoulders and turned *her* palms up and tried to repeat the words after me. She thought it was a language lesson.

"No," I said. "We've got to find them." I pointed to the forest.

She thought shrugging and turning her palms up was a new dance of some kind, I guess, because she began to audition, looking to me for approval.

I said, "Look — please! We're in trouble. Will you kindly

144

get with it? *Die Tie! Pie!* They're out in the forest somewhere."

I made violent motions and she stopped, and her bright
eyes got even brighter. She laughed and ran toward the
trees.

It was a big lift for me. I'd finally gotten to her and the
search was on. The forest was Gina's home, and there was
no doubt in my mind that she could lead me to Doc Tom
and Pete.

I followed her in, and any earlier rough going was like
walking down a highway compared to what followed.
Places where she slipped through easily, even with her
sarong on, grew teeth and gnawed at me as I passed.

My clothes were ripped, and I looked as though I'd been
attacked by a dozen ravenous cats when, half an hour
later, we broke through into the most beautiful little sanctuary I'd ever seen.

There was a crystal-clear pool with a small waterfall
feeding it at one end. The bank was covered with soft
green grass and was surrounded by flowers of so many
beautiful shapes and colors that I was dazzled. And to add
to the brilliance of the place, there were schools of small
fish in the pond that flashed back more color from the
water.

A Hollywood set decorator couldn't have approached
this place even with an unlimited budget behind him.

As I stood there taking it in, Gina laughed and whipped
off her sarong and dived into the pool. I stared, gaping.
How had she possibly interpreted my attempts to communicate into a desire to go swimming?

Suddenly I realized it hadn't been that way. She

thought I was asking her to find us a hiding place. This was it. But it was the last thing I'd needed at the time, and I was in deeper trouble than before. I doubted if I would ever have been able to find my way back to where the tunnel had arrived, and that made me lost too, right along with Doc Tom and Pete. And worst of all, we were lost in different parts of the jungle.

Gina was swimming like a fish and laughing like some crazy little mermaid as she motioned to me to come into the pool. But I was in no mood. I motioned to her, sternly, to come out. I picked up her sarong where she'd dropped it and laid it at the edge of the pool and pointed to it with a frown on my face.

Then I turned away and began examining some of the gorgeous flowers that hung on all sides of us.

One of them gave me a little jolt. It looked like a beautiful crimson mouth, and when I put my finger into it, that was what it turned out to be: a beautiful crimson mouth. But with teeth that clamped down on my finger and tried to dig in.

I let out a yelp and yerked away, pulling the blossom off its stem and yanking a few of its teeth as I got my finger loose.

And with the mood I was in already, that changed everything for me. It went to prove that a lot of what you see and feel is already in your mind, because I didn't see the place as lovely any more. The flowers became sinister, their heady perfume a dangerous gas, the soft green grass a potential pitfall that might open and swallow me.

I saw the whole place as a gaudy deathtrap.

And Gina? She'd become just plain impossible. A frustrating burden I was carrying on my back.

She had her sarong on when I turned around, and she was looking at me with disappointment in her eyes. What she'd done hadn't pleased me, and so her day was ruined.

I felt guilty, but of what I didn't quite know. I only knew I had to get back to the open country. Maybe that wasn't the right answer, but nothing good was going to happen where we were. That was for sure.

So I tried again. I made a big circle in the air and jumped through it. I pointed to the flowers and made the circle again.

This she understood, and the doubt cleared from her questioning eyes. She knew what I wanted: to go where the rainbow ring was. And we started back as we'd come.

I'd taken off my jacket when we came to the pool, and as I was putting it back on, my hand hit the pocket and I realized I still had Dad's letter. But we were on the move again, so I left it for later.

We made the trek back. And half an hour later I went from the bottom to the absolute top. I went through the jungle literally dragging my spirits behind me.

Then, as I stepped into the open, I started running like a fool, yelling, "Dad! Dad!" And not caring if every native in the forest heard me.

He was standing there where the tunnel had been, looking around like a man who had just arrived in a strange town.

Jungle Battle

WE BOTH underplayed it. After that first dash I made in his direction and one quick clinch, I grinned and said, "Welcome to — somewhere. Your guess is as good as mine."

"Where are Tom and Pete?"

"They got lost."

"Where?"

I knew what he meant. A million years away? A hundred thousand? "Right here, somewhere. In that jungle. They'll show up."

That last was my contribution to the calm outlook. I didn't have any idea whether they would show up or not. Dad was still looking things over.

"Shouldn't we find cover? Are there any hostiles around?"

"There are hostiles, but I think we're better off here than in the jungle. If they come, I'd rather meet them in the open."

There was so much that each of us had to tell the other that neither of us knew where to start. Dad looked at Gina, who was standing nearby with a smile that said she wanted to be a part of this but didn't know how.

"I see you've found a friend," Dad said.

"Uh-huh. I guess I've acquired a kind of little sister. Or maybe a cousin. We don't communicate very well, but she's really sharp."

Gina knew we were talking about her, and she wanted to get into the act — definitely wanted to please. And she picked a pretty sensational way of trying. With a flashing smile at Dad, she pointed to me, then took off her sarong, and held it out. She pointed at it proudly and then pointed at me.

Dad blinked, and I'd never been so embarrassed in my life. I grabbed the sarong and wrapped it around her and said, "Keep your clothes on," very sharply.

She was surprised and a little hurt as she tied the thing back on again. I tried to explain to Dad.

"The people here are backward in some things. I made this Paris creation for her. She was just trying to explain that —"

Dad laughed. "I understand." But then he was all business again. "What can we do about finding Tom and Pete?"

"I don't know. We were trapped in a native village back

149

there and all escaped together. They shouldn't be far away."

"How long ago?"

"A couple of hours."

"They were expecting me to arrive, of course."

"Well, no —"

"The letter didn't come?"

"It came, but we haven't had a chance to read it yet."

This really floored him. "H'mmm. In a situation like this, I'd think mail from home would be important."

"It was, Dad, but things have been pretty hectic."

Our conversation wasn't being carried on under the most ideal circumstances. The grass wasn't high enough to hide in, and we'd each dropped to one knee facing each other, our rifles braced on the ground and gripped in tight fists. And we didn't look at each other as we talked, but over each other's shoulders, scanning the forest line.

I expected a herd of spear and club carriers to come charging out at any moment, and Dad was not blind to the situation.

Only Gina was calm and relaxed. She dropped down into the grass, and her eyes kept moving back and forth as she watched us and tried to understand.

"My prayers were answered when I found you here," Dad said. "The worst, at our end, was not knowing. You could all have been dead or irretrievably lost. We worked like madmen to repair the unit, always wondering if anything would ever come of it. It was the not knowing."

I forgot the jungle for a few moments and looked into his face. It reflected the strain he'd been under. There were dark circles under his eyes, and he was pale and drawn.

"Dad, it was a miracle, the way you repaired the unit."

His smile was faint. "My conscience was a whiplash driving me on. After it was too late, I realized that I'd risked precious lives through my own greed for success. I let Tom go too quickly. Before the bugs were out of the machine. When it was necessary for someone to go after him, the first error made the second necessary. It was all my responsibility. Gabe and Lee and Dave were fantastic. We all just quit sleeping."

I saw something move in the trees. "Watch it," I said. "I think we've got company."

Dad turned and looked. There were two dark faces there now, then three and four. I identified them as the tribe that had attacked the village. They'd all worn the same red paint design on one cheek. Otherwise, during the fight, they wouldn't have known who was killing whom.

"You know more about the situation than I do, Bob. If they attack, do we do the obvious thing?"

"Defend ourselves, you mean? I guess we do."

"They're over two hundred yards away. Their intentions should be pretty clear by the time they get here."

"They don't seem to be afraid of guns, but if we started dropping them they might get the idea."

Actually Gina gave us the sign. She came close and crouched beside me, and she wasn't smiling any more. Her reaction told us they were there to kill.

Neither Dad nor I made any mention of our greatest fear: that Doc Tom and Pete were already dead.

Then I thought of something I'd been stupid not to think of before, and I felt better. "They're still alive and safe," I said.

"How can you be sure?"

"Because there have been no rifle shots. I would have heard them. And Doc Tom and Pete wouldn't go down without firing a shot. I'm sure they would have gotten in some action with their .45's."

"Unless they were overwhelmed too quickly."

"The chances are slim. They were aware of the situation."

The faces disappeared and I glanced at Gina, who had turned and was looking the other way. She pointed in that direction and Dad frowned at me, his eyes questioning.

"I think she means they'll surround us."

And almost immediately some faces appeared on that side, but they too disappeared.

"What does it mean?" Dad asked. "Why don't they attack? You said they weren't afraid of our guns."

"We can only guess. Maybe they're waiting for more warriors to show up. The ones we saw might be an advance party — scouts."

"We've made some improvements on the machine I didn't get a chance to tell you about." His tired eyes scanned the forest line. "If I'd only had the sense to wait a little while. None of this would have happened."

"What improvements, Dad?"

"All the arrival uncertainty is gone." He showed me a small, compact black box that he could hold in the palm of his hand. "With this I can create a guide channel and

send a signal. It was made possible when we found a way
to channel in far more power than before."

"It sounds pretty complicated."

"It is. The best way to understand it is to think of a
pilot light on a gas stove. Always there, ready and waiting
to be hit with a gas stream. There is a 'pilot light' back
in the laboratory. I have only to touch it with a signal
from this unit and the tunnel is activated. In a sense it
comes hunting for this unit — and finds it.

"It's piracy, in a sense, also," Dad said gravely. "I had
to usurp several very strong patents, held by big corporations. But I couldn't wait for permissions that would never
have been given."

"I'd think the corporations would have been happy to
cooperate."

Dad shook his head. "There are vast complications in
this time-travel business. You'll remember we started out
to find a way to offset gravity. Time travel as an estab-
lished practice faces staggering problems — political, so-
cial, ethical. I'm convinced that regardless of the speed
with which the world has advanced, it is not yet ready for
pioneering in this direction. The whole concept is too
frightening."

I grabbed Dad's shoulder. "Did you hear that? It
sounded like someone yelling."

"I heard it."

The sound had come faintly, but there was no doubt
about the next sound. A pistol shot. And another.

Dad turned. "It came from that direction."

The sounds were growing louder — coming toward us —
and we felt helpless standing there listening to them.

"It has to be Doc Tom and Pete."

"Maybe we should go and help them," Dad said.

"I'll go. You stay here."

"No." Dad raised his rifle and fired it. "We'll stay here and try to signal them in the right direction. If we went to them, it would just be four of us blundering around in the jungle."

That made sense. I raised my own rifle and fired a shot. "They're coming closer."

Gina crouched quietly on the ground close to my feet. There was an alertness about her. I got the feeling she was ready to move instantly and swiftly in any direction. Like a deer at bay.

The faces of the natives appeared again on both sides of us. As we watched, some fifty or sixty of them moved into the open.

The showdown was close.

I fired my rifle again and Dad checked the hand-sized unit.

I said, "They seem to be waiting until they can take us all at once."

"Maybe the ones after Tom and Pete are a different tribe, and the ones with the red paint are confused."

"Could be."

Then Doc Tom and Pete broke into the open, and we were in the middle of an attack. Their clothes were torn and we could see blood, but neither of them appeared to be badly wounded. A dozen natives followed them into the opening, yelling and chattering and waving spears. More natives appeared on all sides, and they began circling in.

Dad punched a button on the unit and then stuck it into his belt. "We've got to hold the flanks back until they get here," he said. "You take the left."

There were no doubts now. We had to fight.

Maybe I felt a little squeamish, firing into that advancing line, but I don't think so. Self-preservation is a strong instinct. I raised my rifle and fired, and one of the warriors dropped. I heard Dad's rifle crack at the same moment.

A few of the warriors slowed up and looked at their fallen comrades, but they didn't seem to associate their death with our rifles.

Four guns were firing as Doc Tom and Pete stopped to pick off two pursuers who were close. That seemed to have some effect on the others. Most of them stopped and stared, chattering at each other.

But the two wings were coming in. They would reach us at about the same time as Doc Tom and Pete. I dropped two more, wishing to heaven that they'd get the idea. It did slow them down a little, but they kept coming. Several spears were thrown, but they fell short.

Then, destiny favoring us in the matter of timing, the rainbow ring appeared.

It came in bright and strong, and a half dozen of the red-spotted warriors, close enough to cut Doc Tom and Pete off, stopped dead, the whites of their eyes showing in sudden fear.

"Come on!" Dad yelled. "Hurry. You can make it!"

Doc Tom was close to exhaustion. We could only surmise what had happened in the jungle, but it had been plenty rough, no doubt about that. He dropped his rifle and staggered toward the tunnel.

Dad pushed him through and then fired in a group of warriors who'd decided the tunnel was something to attack. Even as I hit another one in the leg, I had to admire his courage.

Dad had to push Pete into the ring. Pete had hesitated and was set to help fend off the warriors. When Dad grabbed my arm, I got tough and turned him around and pushed him through the ring.

Two of the natives jumped at me as I dived in after him, and one of them hurled a spear.

The natives didn't make it, holding back, I suppose, as they saw me vanish. The spear made it though. It came straight at me.

Then . . .

. . . it hissed past my shoulder and skidded across the floor of the laboratory.

We were home!

But there was a complication. As the ring vanished, I thought about Gina. Had she been killed? I felt guilty at having forgotten her because she had put her trust in me.

Suddenly I saw her. She was on the floor, huddled against the wall on the side of the laboratory opposite the control panel. Her eyes were wide and staring, and there was fear in them.

Monster in the Driveway

THE REST OF IT happened pretty fast and was a kind of coming together of several things in a way that made me think later. And after giving it some thought, I decided destiny must have written the end to satisfy herself — that is, if destiny is a *she*.

Anyhow, my first concern was about Gina. Her face was filled with terror. She was so scared that she didn't even have the courage to run to me for protection.

Pete and Doc Tom had dropped to the floor in one corner, perfect pictures of exhaustion. Dad had turned his attention to the machine, going into conference with Gabe and Lee and Dave without stopping to say "hello."

I realized from the way they acted that there were problems. I heard Gabe say, "We overestimated the power charge. It's not draining off." And I could vaguely feel the supercharged air around me as I ran to Gina.

I took her hand and smiled at her. "It's all right," I said. "Everything is all right."

It wasn't hard to realize what she was going through. First, she was only a savage; and second, she'd been hurled with violence into a terrible world she couldn't begin to understand.

I hadn't seen her go through the ring, but that didn't matter now. She was here. Her eyes were still big, and her fear so great that at first she jerked her hand away from mine.

I took it again, very gently, and kept on smiling. "It's all right," I kept saying. "Don't worry. You're safe now." I was speaking words she didn't understand, but trying to put the assurance into the tone of my voice.

I lifted her to her feet and she stood there, her eyes beginning to move, covering the laboratory as though she saw it as a great monster that had swallowed her.

I thought I'd better get her out of there, and that turned out to be my mistake.

Slowly, gently, I led her toward the door out into the yard, figuring that when she got out there she would see familiar things — trees, grass, flowers. And it might have worked except that destiny — or chance — decreed otherwise.

As I opened the door, still talking to her, I heard Dad say, "We'll have to activate the tunnel again. It's the only quick way to drain off the power. Otherwise we'll have an explosion here."

Gabe said, "Somebody better stand by in case someone or something comes through."

"O.K.," Lee said. "Hand me that rifle."

By that time I'd opened the door, and Gina and I had stepped outside.

But some truck driver chose that moment to make a delivery. He was out in the street, and he swung his big red delivery truck into the drive and came toward the laboratory.

I felt Gina's hand tighten in mine. I looked and saw the terror in her face as she saw what she could only think of as some great, terrible monster bearing down on her.

She screamed and jerked away, and lunged back through the door. I started after her, but she moved like a darting hummingbird, straight toward the rainbow ring that had now been activated. In this terrible new world *that* was the only thing that she was in the least familiar with — that she even vaguely understood. It was sanctuary.

And she plunged through it and disappeared.

I charged after her, but as I reached the platform Dad was there to stop me.

"No, Bob, let her go. I'm sorry, but it's best."

"Those natives back there! She'll land right in the middle of —"

"No, she won't."

Gabe had been ignoring everything but the control and dial panel. As the signal came that he was looking for, he jerked two switches and deactivated the ring. It faded.

"But they'll still be there," I said. "They'll kill her."

"It won't arrive in exactly the same spot. It will be at least five hundred yards away."

"O.K.," I said. "I guess there's nothing we can do about it anyhow."

Dad turned back to the ticklish work of finally quieting

the tunnel and the high-voltage power that made it possible. I moved toward the door and an overpowering thought hit me. A crazy thought in a way:

The girl I'd just seen run screaming toward the tunnel had been dead for at least 20,000 years. The whole world had changed. The world I'd seen her rush back to wasn't even there!

Weird, illogical thoughts, but there they were. I looked at my hand. Only a few moments before it had gripped hers.

But what it had gripped had been less than dust for ages.

I didn't like this line of thinking, and tried to veer away from it. It only proved that nothing is at all the way we see it and conceive it. Science had proved that again and again.

And with our time tunnel we had repeated that proof. Two and two was four and not four. It was only four when it was not something else.

"Maybe we're proving things too fast," I thought.

But I knew that wasn't true. It was our job to prove things. And we would have to keep right on trying. Although I didn't think we would go back in time again. Not from what Dad had said.

But I had the memory of all of it.

And of little Gina.

And I hoped she would remember me.